THE
RAINBOW'S
END

Books by Robert Funderburk

THE INNOCENT YEARS

Love and Glory
These Golden Days
Heart and Soul
Old Familiar Places
Tenderness and Fire
The Rainbow's End

DYLAN ST. JOHN NOVEL

The Fires of Autumn
All the Days Were Summer

9706

THE RAINBOW'S END

ROBERT FUNDERBURK

BETHANY HOUSE PUBLISHERS
MINNEAPOLIS, MINNESOTA 55438

The Rainbow's End
Copyright © 1997
Robert W. Funderburk

Cover illustration by Joe Nordstrom

Published by Bethany House Publishers
A Ministry of Bethany Fellowship, Inc.
11300 Hampshire Avenue South
Minneapolis, Minnesota 55438

Printed in the United States of America.

Library of Congress Cataloging-in-Publication Data

CIP Data applied for

ISBN 1–55661–465–9   CIP

To
The Istrouma Senior Class of 1960
and
Those long-ago, lovely "Innocent Years"

ROBERT FUNDERBURK is the author of the DYLAN ST. JOHN NOVELS and THE INNOCENT YEARS series with Bethany House Publishers. Much of the research for both series was gained through growing up in Baton Rouge and then working as a Louisiana state probation and parole officer for twenty years. He and his wife have one daughter and live in Louisiana.

CONTENTS

★ ★ ★

PART FOUR
CLOSE TO THE HEART

PART ONE
★ ★ ★

THE SAD AND LOVELY YEARS

ONE

A MODEST MADNESS

★ ★ ★

"How many times do you get to see a governor hauled off to the loony bin?" Cassidy Temple's blue eyes held the intense light that always presaged a sudden and joyous veering away from the ordinary.

"You're awful, Cassidy Temple!" Kay Starnes, a frown troubling her heart-shaped face, sat next to Cassidy in the front seat of his father's '39 Ford coupe. "We shouldn't be doing this. It's just not . . . respectful." She smoothed out the wrinkles in her straight skirt and adjusted the collar of her plum-colored blouse as though neatness could perhaps substitute for respect.

Driving in front of the City Club past the great live oaks lining North Boulevard, Cassidy pulled in behind a white '56 Chevy wagon with the WLCS call letters on its doors. He watched the driver speaking into his microphone as he trailed a big gray Oldsmobile, allegedly transporting the governor of Louisiana to the East Baton Rouge Parish Coroner's Office. Turning the radio dial to ninety-one, Cassidy adjusted the volume. *According to a reliable source, the governor's recent erratic behavior prompted his family to have him submit to a medical examination.*

' "If 'Uncle Earl' wanted respect he shouldn't act so nutty all the time." Cassidy turned right on St. Ferdinand toward the district court building that housed the coroner's office. "I think all he ever wanted was to be governor and have a good time doing it."

"He knows how to have a good time all right. Blaze Starr could tell us a thing or two about that."

Kay turned toward the backseat. "You can just hush that kind of talk around me, Caffey!"

At seventeen, Caffey Sams weighed two hundred and twenty pounds and was still filling out his six-foot, three-inch frame. His wiry red hair seldom felt the touch of a comb's teeth. The distance most people kept from him gave mute testimony to his intimidating appearance, as well as the fact that he had only a passing acquaintance with soap and water. "Sorry. Sometimes I forget when one of Cass's girls—I mean, when you're around, Kay."

" 'One of'!" Kay stared at Cass's clean profile. "What does he mean by that?"

A tomcat grin spread across Cassidy's face as he glanced at her. "He's just pulling your leg, darling. You know you're the only girl in my life."

Doubt flickered in Kay's light brown eyes, almost the exact color as her short hair. "I hope you're not just stringing me along, Cass."

But Cassidy's mind had already turned away from Kay's concerns about their relationship. "Look, they're pulling into the lot behind the courthouse." He pulled over to the curb and parked behind the white station wagon. "Wait here. I'm gonna find out what's going on."

"Let me go with you." Caffey lurched forward, pushing against the seat.

"No." The sound of Cassidy's voice abruptly stopped him. "Stay with Kay. I'll be right back."

Caffey's look of disappointment served as his only response. He plopped back against the seat, crossing his arms over his massive chest.

Cassidy saw the big Oldsmobile pulling down the concrete ramp that led to the basement of the courthouse. He walked across the parking lot toward an already gathering crowd of reporters, courthouse employees, three or four uniformed policemen, and the merely curious who had wandered off the streets.

Cassidy walked over to a man in his mid-thirties, dressed in wrinkled gray trousers and a blue seersucker jacket with stained lapels. "What's going on?"

The man stopped scribbling on his note pad. "Chester's gonna come down and take a look at the governor. That's what I heard, anyway."

Cassidy watched the Oldsmobile ease down the ramp and out of sight. The reporter pushed through the crowd, holding his press card in front of him. Following him, Cassidy was abruptly stopped by the outstretched arm of a burly policeman.

"That's far enough, little boy." The sergeant glowered down at Cassidy. "You just hold it right here."

Cassidy's eyes sparked with anger at the officer's words, but he had learned to control his temper when all the odds were against him . . . most of the time. Two minutes later the harried reporter pushed his way back through the crowd, scratching notes on his pad as he walked.

"What happened?"

The reporter glanced up at Cassidy. "Chester gave him one of his thorough examinations."

"Who?"

"Chester Williams, the coroner."

"Oh yeah." Cassidy recognized the name but had never associated it with the man's position. "You mean he's already finished with the governor?"

The man glanced down at his watch and continued writing. "Yep."

"What did he do?"

The reporter stopped writing and scowled at Cassidy. "I usually ask the questions." His face registered a faint recognition. "Don't I know you?"

"You ever write for the sports section?"

"Sometimes."

"I run track for Istrouma. Won state in the hundred last year." Cassidy watched the man slowly nod his head and smile. "Gonna win it again this year, too."

"I remember you now. You're Dalton Temple's little brother. Whatever happened to him?"

Cassidy winced slightly when the reporter referred to him as Dalton's little brother. "Went down to New Orleans."

"I believe you just might win the hundred again this year." The man rested his pencil point on the note pad. "Don't know how I could have missed that white hair of yours. You can really fly. What was your time . . . nine point nine?"

"Nine eight."

"What're you hanging around here for?"

"Wanted to see what was happening."

"Well, ol' Chester walked over to the car down there," the reporter nodded toward the ramp entrance, "looked in, and said, 'He looks crazy to me.'

14

And that's all there was to it."

"That's it?"

The man started writing again.

"What happens now?"

"They're gonna take ol' Earl on down to the mental hospital at Mandeville."

"Right now?"

"See for yourself." The reporter motioned behind him with his thumb.

Cassidy watched the gray car backing slowly out of the courthouse basement, the policemen clearing a path through the onlookers. Two motorcycle officers, their high black boots gleaming in the bright May sunshine, provided the escort for Louisiana's latest political disaster in the making.

Racing across the parking lot, Cassidy noticed the driver of the WLCS station wagon still speaking into his mike. He ran around his father's car to the driver's side, snatched the door open, and leaped behind the wheel.

"What's going on?" Caffey leaned forward, his mouth agape, showing the dark gap where as a child he had lost his left eyetooth to one of his father's drunken rages.

"They're taking him down to Mandeville." Cassidy started the engine, slipped the Ford into first gear, and again fell in behind the Chevy following the governor.

"We can't go to Mandeville!"

"Why not?" Cassidy snapped.

"Just . . . just because." Kay seemed incapable of adjusting to Cassidy's seemingly irrational decisions.

Cassidy gunned the engine, keeping his third-place position in the impromptu parade as it raced down America Street, turning left at the rear of the governor's mansion. "Ah, they're just taking him home." But the Oldsmobile screeched around the corner toward North Boulevard and turned right. Cassidy's face brightened as he eased down on the Ford's accelerator. "No, they're not. Hot dog! Here we go!"

With the tires whining against the pavement as he made the turn onto North Boulevard, Cassidy held the steering wheel with both hands, then switched back to one as the chase straightened out into a dead run. Ahead of him the sirens on the motorcycles screamed a clear path through the city. When the speedometer reached thirty-five, he slapped the gearshift up into second.

"Cassidy, please stop! You can't keep up with them," Kay pleaded, her voice rising in fear.

Gunning the engine, Cassidy slouched easily behind the wheel. "You won't believe how fast this ol' wreck is. They used cars like this to run moonshine in Mississippi." Noticing the man in the WLCS Chevy had put his mike away, he glanced over at Kay's pale face, then flicked the volume knob on the radio. At sixty-five he jerked the gearshift down into third as the latest "Top Forty" hit blasted the car's interior.

Hey, Mama, don't treat me wrong.

"This is fun!" Caffey placed both hands on the back of the seat, his gap-toothed smile bright on his face, as plain and broad as a board fence.

"Yeah," Cassidy agreed, grinning at Kay, his blue eyes touched with wildness. "Sure beats sitting in Mrs. Kendrick's English class, don't it?"

"Slow down, Cass." Kay's voice held an edge of hysteria. "Please!"

Cassidy watched the Oldsmobile, followed by the white Chevy, turn left on Nineteenth Street. He touched the brake, shoving the gearshift up into second to take the turn. "You wouldn't want to miss this, Kay. This is history!"

Sirens wailed ahead of them as the motorcycles cleared traffic on Florida, heading east between two fences, one of iron and one of stone, bordering cemeteries that predated the Civil War. Reaching the long, straight stretch of four-lane, the Oldsmobile picked up speed.

When Cassidy screeched around the corner onto Florida, the big car had already gained a quarter mile on him. "Gonna be tough to keep up now."

"You can do it, Cass!" Caffey had become a one-man backseat cheering section.

Cassidy watched the Chevy pull over into the right lane, giving up the chase. "I figured that little six-cylinder engine wouldn't last much longer."

Suddenly the sirens sounded much louder. Caffey turned around and gazed out the back window. "You gonna have to give it up, Cass."

"Why?" Cassidy glanced at the speedometer, rocking on ninety-five. "We're gaining on them."

Caffey turned around and leaned forward. "Yeah, but somebody's gaining on us."

Glancing into the rearview mirror, Cassidy saw the flashing red light on top of a city police unit. "Always got to be somebody trying to spoil my fun." He grunted in anger, then let off the accelerator and braked toward the side of the street.

★ ★ ★

A thin, bright scimitar moon hung in the dark sky far, far above the swamps and marshes and wooded uplands of South Louisiana. Down below, the Amite River swirled and gurgled around and over a fallen

17

tree, making soft music on its winding way to Lake Ponchartrain.

Sixteen- and seventeen-year-olds crowded the white sand beach of the river located on the fringes of Baton Rouge. Despite all their differences, they had dedicated themselves to the common proposition that all the summer days and nights of 1959 had been expressly created for them to enjoy to the fullest extent of their youthful vigor and foolishness.

Several bonfires dotted the expanse of sand, their flames whipping like torn cloth in the night wind. Car radios tuned to the same station played identical songs against the backdrop of sand and water and trees. Some of the girls, caught in the flickering light of the fires, danced in the sand to the pounding beat of the music. The boys stood in groups of three or four talking in undertones, waiting for a slow song, or slouched against car fenders trying to smoke their cigarettes like James Dean.

Hey, Bird Dog, get away from my chick . . .

"Why do girls like to dance to that kind of music?" Caffey, his wrinkled gray trousers stained with grease from the makeshift mechanic shop that was part of his house, watched Kay and several of her friends scuffing sand in time with the music.

"If you can figure out why girls do *anything*, you be sure to tell me first." Cassidy's skin, tanned to a bronze color during the four-month track season, contrasted with his hair. His faded Levi's and white polo shirt hung loosely on his five-ten, one hundred and fifty-five-pound frame as he slouched against the fender of his father's Ford, a Camel cigarette dangling from his lips.

Caffey sat down in the sand, leaning back against the white sidewall tire. "I don't even understand that song." His lower jaw sagged and a glazed look came into his brown eyes. "Johnny's a joker, and he's a dog . . . and the teacher's pet. What's all that supposed to mean?"

"Don't make it too complicated, Caffey. All it's about is somebody trying to steal somebody else's girlfriend, and he doesn't like it very much."

"Oh." Caffey grinned up at his friend and mentor. "That's kinda funny, then."

"Maybe not."

Cassidy gazed at the dancers dressed in jeans and summer blouses, their loafers and white socks scattered in the sand next to the fire. The night wind made a sighing sound in the tops of the sycamores and sweet gum trees. Couples had begun pairing off for the night. They sat near the bonfires or walked hand in hand along the water's edge. One lone radio remained tuned to the station that stayed on all night.

Put your head on my shoulder . . .

"Wanna dance?" Kay, still breathing hard from her sand and music exercise, strolled over to Cassidy. "That's our song playing, isn't it?"

Cassidy had no idea it was their song. Sometime in April he had found himself "going steady" with Kay without knowing how it had come about. He stared at her—pretty, smart, and possessing that all-important trait for any seventeen-year-old girl, a "good personality." And he suddenly started to feel as though she was fitting him slowly and tenderly into a handmade velvet-lined, lace-trimmed straitjacket. "I guess it is our song . . . if you say it is, sweetheart."

A shadow of a frown flickered across Kay's face. "You mean you don't remember the time—"

"Sure I do," Cassidy interrupted her, pushing off the fender and stepping toward her. He slipped his arm around her slender waist, took her hand in his, and pulled her close. "Now, all you have to do is," he sang the rest, "put your head on my shoulll . . . der."

Kay nestled against him, moving slowly across the sand almost in time with the music. "I do love you so much, Cass. Wouldn't it be wonderful if we could stay like this forever?"

Cassidy felt a strap on the straitjacket pulling tight across his back. "Yeah." He glanced at Caffey, staring up at the sky, still sitting with his back against the Ford's tire. "Hey, Caffey. Come on and dance with us."

Caffey looked up at them, the smile on his face that of a child in spite of his bulk. "Nah. You know I don't know nothin' about that kinda stuff."

Taking his hand away from Kay's, Cassidy motioned to Caffey. "C'mon, we'll teach you. It's easy."

"Well, okay then." Caffey stood up, brushing the sand from his stained trousers, his grin wider than ever. "You sure it's all right with you, Kay?"

Kay gave Cassidy a look of mild exasperation, then smiled at Caffey. "Sure, c'mon. It'll be fun."

The three of them—a soft, sweet-smelling girl; a bulky, good-natured giant; and a lean, rebellious sprinter—slogged together through the sand to the sound of Paul Anka's youthful voice beneath the star-crowded summer sky. The song ended, and the unlikely trio stopped their dance and walked over to the bonfire. After two minutes of the DJ's raucous commercials, Johnny Mathis's soulful version of "Misty" drifted on the mild night air.

"I'm gonna get a beer."

Kay took Cassidy's arm and frowned. "I wish you wouldn't."

"Why not?" He started across the sand toward the car. "I've only had two all night. Want one, Caffey?"

20

Caffey shook his head and stared down at his scuffed brown brogans.

Kay watched Cassidy walking out of the firelight into the shadows where the car was parked not far from the dirt road that led through the woods to the beach. "There are times when I wish Cassidy was more like you, Caffey."

A look of mild shock crossed Caffey's broad face. "Really! How come?"

"Well," Kay mused out loud, the tip of her forefinger resting against the side of her smooth chin, "I think because you're not as . . . restless. I guess that's it. Cassidy always seems so dissatisfied and . . . restless."

Caffey shrugged. "If you say so."

Kay sat down next to the fire, crossing her legs Indian fashion. "You've been friends for a long time, haven't you?"

Slumping down on the sand, Caffey rested his massive forearms on his knees. "Yep. Since the fifth grade. We got in this big fight on the first day of school and"—he shrugged his big, rounded shoulders—"I reckon you could say we've been best friends ever since."

"That's how you got to be friends . . . fighting each other." Kay shook her head slowly back and forth. "I don't think I'll ever understand men." She glanced at Cassidy disappearing into the darkness behind the Ford.

Cassidy opened the trunk and lifted the lid on his Thermos ice chest. Reaching inside, he pulled a green-and-white can of Dixie beer from the ice and water, then took a "churchkey" from the floor and punched two holes on opposite sides of the wet can. Lifting it up, he drank three big swallows.

"Got another one in there?"

Cassidy spun around. She was about five six and her straight black hair hung down almost to her waist. In the faint flickering of the bonfires, her eyes were dark pools in her slightly elongated face. She wore sandals, white shorts, and a black knit pullover.

"I might," he said, trying to act as though she hadn't startled him.

"Well . . ." she said in a husky voice that spoke of a close relationship with cigarettes and alcohol. Her full lips curved in a smile as she held her hand out.

"You sure you're old enough?"

"I'm twenty-one. That's legal, isn't it?"

"Depends on what you want to do."

She laughed softly. "Just have a beer for now."

Cassidy pulled out another beer, punched holes in the top, and handed it to her. "What's your name?"

"Betty Jo."

He took her hand. It felt warm, even though the night coolness had set in. "Cassidy."

She took a swallow of beer, then another. "Hmm . . . nice and cold. Best thing I've had all day."

Cassidy stepped aside and closed the trunk. Glancing over his shoulder, he saw Kay and Caffey still sitting by the fire. "What's this all about?"

Betty Jo smiled lazily. "It's about the bluest eyes I've ever seen in my life."

Cassidy felt a warmth rising up his neck, glad for the shadowy darkness that hid his embarrassment. "It's too dark to tell what color anybody's eyes are."

"I've seen you before."

"Oh yeah?" Pride laced liberally with arrogance siphoned off Cassidy's brief fling with embarrassment. "I think I'd remember if we'd met before."

"Track meets," she said enigmatically. "I love to

watch the boys out at LSU run. I'm graduating this year with a degree in English, but sometimes I go to the high school meets." She took another swallow of beer. "You run like a deer. It's almost . . . pretty the way you run."

"Pretty. . . . First time I've ever heard anybody say that about running."

Betty Jo stepped closer to him, her fingertips brushing across the top of his hand. "Stick around me awhile and you might hear a lot of things you've never heard before."

Cassidy couldn't stop the grin that spread across his face. He glanced over his shoulder again.

"You worried about your girlfriend?"

"Not a bit."

"Let's go for a ride, then."

"They came with me. I can't just leave them."

Betty Jo nodded toward a yellow Corvette convertible parked next to the dirt road. "We'll go in my car." She glanced at the couple seated by the fire. "Don't worry. I'll bring you back."

"I've got a better idea."

"Oh yeah?"

Cassidy blocked out a twinge of guilt. "Yeah. I'll leave the keys and let Caffey bring her home."

Betty Jo drained her beer, tossed the can behind her, and slipped her arm inside Cassidy's. "Sounds like you've done this sort of thing before."

Setting his beer can on the Ford's trunk, Cassidy placed his keys next to it, then scrunched across the sand toward Betty Jo's Corvette. "Not me. I'm just overcome by the bad influence of a college girl."

Betty Jo's husky laughter drifted upward toward the bright scimitar moon.

TWO

Knight Templar

★ ★ ★

On November 20, 1959, Istrouma whipped its arch rival Baton Rouge High by a score of fourteen to seven, then went on to win the state championship for the fourth time in five years. But somehow a victory over Baton Rouge High always tasted sweeter even than a state championship, and Hopper's Drive-in was the traditional place to celebrate it.

Cassidy turned the Ford at the break in the neutral ground on Florida Street and pulled into the bumper-to-bumper line of cars entering and leaving Hopper's U-shaped driveway. As they idled around the building, Kay called out the window to her friends. Caffey sat quiet and smiling in the backseat.

"You didn't stand a chance tonight." Kay, wearing Cassidy's red-and-white letter jacket, called out to one of her friends wearing the loser's green-and-gold colors.

The blond girl's smiling face showed no sign of defeat as she yelled back, "Just wait till next year."

"Five years in a row we beat 'em and she's still looking forward to next year." Cassidy, wearing his faded Levi's and black leather jacket, slouched at the wheel, his gaze taking in the not-quite-controlled bedlam of a Hopper's Friday night. "You gotta admire that kind of guts."

Chevys and Fords, a scattering of Studebakers and boxy Plymouths, a few '40s vintage pickups, and one sparkling new Edsel filled all the parking spaces along the curved drive. Teenagers yelled from car to car, strolled across the driveway to the sound of honking horns, threaded their way among the parked cars, or spilled into and out of the neon glare of the white stucco building. The outside speakers blared the Chordettes bouncy, bubbly rendition of "Lollipop."

"Hey, there's one!" Caffey called out from the backseat. "He's leaving now."

Cassidy hit the brakes, letting a white Chevy Corvair back out of the space, then he pulled forward, backed in, and cut his engine and headlights. "Good thing you had your eyes open, Caffey. I woulda missed it and we wouldn't have found another place till next Christmas."

Caffey beamed his pleasure from the backseat. "I'm hungry. Let's eat."

"You're always hungry." Cassidy took a pack of Camels from his jacket, tapped one free, and placed it between his lips. Replacing the pack, he flipped the lid open on his lighter with one hand and flicked it into flame.

"Do you have to smoke, Cass?" Kay's bright smile slipped downward a quarter inch as she spoke. "You know how it always makes me cough inside a car like this."

"Yes, ma'am." Cassidy tucked the lighter inside his

26

jacket but let the cigarette dangle from his lips.

"What'll it be, folks?" A gangly red-haired boy with a short crew cut and freckles sprinkled like confetti across his thin face leaned on the window.

"Caffey, what're you having?"

"Two cheeseburgers, fries, and a chocolate malt." Caffey spit out his order, then his voice dropped a decibel and slowed to a crawl. "But I don't have no money."

"I'll give you a loan till you sell your dog."

"But I ain't got no *dog*, neither."

Cassidy gave him a bland look over the back of the seat. "Joke, Caffey. It's supposed to be a joke."

"Oh yeah."

Cassidy glanced at Kay. "Kinda loses something when you have to explain it."

Kay grinned at him. "I'll just have a cherry Coke. I'm too excited to eat."

"You heard the lady," Cassidy said, jerking his thumb toward Caffey, "and the bottomless pit in the backseat."

"Yeah, and what're you havin'?"

Cassidy rolled his lips, shifting the cigarette to the other side of his mouth. "I think I'll just nibble on this Camel for a while if that's all right with you."

"Sure thing." The boy whirled away, sprinting across the drive and into the building to take his place at the order window with the other carhops.

Cassidy gazed idly at the cars passing by. Girls with shiny hair and bright lips were leaning out the windows and yelling at their friends or taunting their enemies. Their boyfriends were hunched over the steering wheels giving their impression of James Dean mumbling some incoherent phrase in *Rebel Without a Cause* or Elvis sneering at the villain in the cafe fight scene from *Loving You.*

Then he saw a pair of tiny dark eyes like buckshot staring at him from the fleshy face they were buried in.

Warren Barbay, with a barrel chest and arms like fence posts, stood five ten and weighed an even two hundred pounds. His neck was as thick as his bullet-shaped, crew-cut head. He had earned his reputation as the toughest fighter of the class of 1950 in the parking lot of the old Hopper's on Scenic Highway and had dragged it around behind him in his drab existence until it was tarnished and torn and ragged. The look in his eyes said he viewed Cassidy Temple as the chance for a shiny new trophy.

Barbay turned, said something to the driver, who stopped the sleek black '49 Mercury, blocking traffic. Then he opened the passenger door and got out, his black T-shirt clinging tightly to his bulging biceps and the corded muscles of his back. After staring at Cassidy for a few seconds, making sure he had the attention of as many onlookers as possible, he stalked over to the Ford. "You're Austin Youngblood's little brother-in-law, ain't you?"

"Cass, l-let's go. Please!" Kay's voice trembled with fear, her words barely audible.

Since his days in elementary school, Cassidy remembered hearing about the legendary fight between Austin and Barbay. Austin, a state champion boxer at Istrouma, had cut the bully of Baton Rouge High to pieces with his left jabs and right crosses until Barbay backed into a wall and somehow landed a big round-house right. Cassidy did not look up at the big man.

"I been hearing about how tough you are since you was a junior high punk."

Caffey leaned forward, whispering in Cassidy's ear.

"Let me out. I'm bigger than he is."

Cassidy stared through the windshield at the traffic passing by. "He'd kill you," he said, his voice lowered so only Caffey and Kay could hear.

"Please, Cass!" Kay's eyes had grown round and bright with fear.

"Is that right?" Barbay's words rumbled just outside the door. "Are you a tough guy?"

"I'm stronger than anybody." Caffey knotted his fists, trembling with anger.

"You ain't mean enough, Caffey." Cassidy turned his head toward the backseat, trying to reason with his friend. "I'm telling you this guy would kill you."

"You wanna step out of that car and let me get a look at you, pretty boy?"

Caffey growled, his eyes narrowed with rage and frustration. "I ain't scared of him!"

Cassidy glanced at the big man's forearms, propped against the window ledge. "I know that." He glanced at Kay, trembling now, then started the engine.

Barbay stepped around to the front of the Ford, standing with his arms crossed over his chest. "What's wrong, pretty boy? You runnin' home to mama?"

Cassidy's eyes filled with a cold, hard light. He killed the engine, leaning slightly forward, his hand slipping beneath the seat, before opening the car door.

"Don't, Cass!" Kay grabbed his arm with both hands, squeezing tightly. "He'll go away."

"No, he won't." He stepped out of the car, watching Barbay back into the center of the driveway.

Traffic had stopped, the line of cars curving back around the building and into Florida Street. Word of the coming fight spread through the crowd like a virus. Cars emptied in a matter of seconds, their occupants gathering in a ragged formation around the open area between the parking area and the building. Everyone inside the building deserted their sundaes and malts and po'boys, spilling out into the brisk November air.

Cassidy glanced at the surging crowd, young faces eager to see the first blow struck. Even the eyes of his friends glittered with the frenzy of the pack, that malevolent gleaming satisfied only by the shedding of blood.

Barbay stood in the center of the driveway, arms still folded over his massive chest, his little eyes glinting like anthracite. "I heard all you Istrouma boys carry little pink lace hankies in your purses." He basked in the wide-eyed adulation of his fans, who had never seen him lose a fight in the nine years since he had dropped Austin with his big right fist.

Cassidy approached cautiously, holding his right hand down and slightly behind his leg. His level gaze never faltered from Barbay as he stopped six feet in front of the big man. They stood the exact height, but Cassidy spotted him forty-five pounds in weight that was mostly bone, muscle, and sinew. Barbay lifted weights at Alvin Roy's Health Studio four days a week, including Christmas day, when Roy would give him a key to get inside the building.

Cassidy, quick, agile, and with lightning reflexes, knew he could outbox Barbay, but the end result would be the same as Austin's as soon as the big man, using his strength and bulk, backed him against the building or against the side of a car and landed that huge roundhouse right.

"What's wrong, pretty boy? You too scared to talk?" Barbay's thick lips pulled back over teeth that carried the dingy color of dried egg yolk.

Cassidy knew Barbay's pattern of fighting, of trying to provoke his opponent, antagonize him into making a stupid mistake in the heat of anger . . . and he made it part of his offensive.

"You ain't gonna wet yore pants now are you, pretty b—Ahh. . . ."

His expression never changing, Cassidy had suddenly taken one step forward and kicked Barbay in the left shin, the hard leather sole of his shoe crunching into the bone. With another bellow of pain and rage, Barbay bent forward from the waist, grabbing his damaged shinbone. Cassidy planted his left foot just to the right of Barbay's head and, using a shoulder turn and the coiled power of his leg and back muscles, unleashed a right cross. His fist, encased in brass knuckles, slammed into the howling man's left temple with a sickening thud.

Barbay's bellowing stopped; his eyes glazed over as though someone had dashed varnish on them. But still he didn't go down . . . and that proved his undoing. Almost unconscious now, operating solely on reflexes, he swung a looping right hand. Cassidy easily ducked under it, stepped forward, and drove his right fist directly into Barbay's jaw. A sound as though someone had broken a stick underwater was followed by Barbay's howl of mortal agony, and his nine-year reign ended.

Cassidy glanced once at his fallen enemy, lying motionless on his back in the center of the driveway. Swelling had begun in Barbay's left temple. His partially closed eyelids flickered slightly, the thin white line of eyeball showing beneath them. A ragged, wheezing breath escaped his nose and mouth.

Staring straight ahead, Cassidy walked directly to

the Ford, got in, and cranked the engine. The crowd gathered around Barbay looked like a freeze frame on a theater screen. As Cassidy eased forward, three of Barbay's friends, expressions of shock on their faces, ran forward and dragged him out of the way. Cassidy drove slowly out of the parking space, down the drive, turning right onto Florida Street. The faint wailing of a siren sounded far off in the chill November night.

★ ★ ★

"How's the novel going?" Wearing Istrouma track shorts and a white T-shirt, Cassidy stood in Sharon's doorway, his hair tousled and damp from the shower.

Sharon turned from her writing desk located in front of a tall window, her fingers resting lightly on the keys of the twenty-five-year-old Royal typewriter that her father had bought for her at one of the shops on Royal Street in the French Quarter. "If I'd known it was going to be this much work, I don't think I would have started the thing." She took a hardback copy of *Doctor Zhivago* from her desktop, slipped it into the bookcase built by her father, and stretched lazily. "I just may give up on it."

Cassidy walked into the room and sat down on the edge of the bed. He stared at his sister, the amber lamplight gleaming on her soft brown hair. Five years back he thought he would lose her, but her leukemia had been in remission for two years now and she looked the picture of health. Remembering her quiet courage during the years of intense pain and blood transfusions, he said softly, "You couldn't give up even if you wanted to."

Sharon's deep blue eyes glistened in the lamplight. "Why couldn't I?"

"'Cause it's just not in you . . . that's why."

"Thanks, Cass. I think I give up on writing at least once a day." Sharon unrolled the sheet of paper from her typewriter and glanced at it. "But you're right. I'm going to finish this novel if it takes the rest of my life."

Cassidy gazed at the bookcase packed with novels and books of poetry by America's best writers. "I wonder if all of them found writing was hard work."

Sharon stared thoughtfully at her younger brother. "I suppose so. There's no easy way to do it. You just have to sit down and grind it out."

"What. . . ? No sudden inspiration in the middle of the night . . . no jumping out of bed and frantically typing out fifty pages of pure genius?"

Laughing softly, Sharon said, "Hollywood, Cass. That's pure Hollywood."

"You gonna tell me what your book's about?"

Sharon grinned, then launched into her best Jimmy Cagney impersonation. "It's about this blond-haired kid, see. Yeah. The boy comes from a good family, but he's always getting into fights, see. He grows up, but he keeps fighting like he was still a kid, see. Yeah."

Cassidy tried to stop the grin that was spreading across his face but couldn't.

Sharon added Cagney's sneer to her performance, wrinkling her nose, her top lip lifted, revealing straight white teeth. "One day the coppers get after him, see, and they got tommy guns, see. Then they start—"

"All right," Cassidy interrupted her, then burst into a fit of laughter. When he could control himself, he said, "I think I get the picture."

"I don't think you do, Cass." Sharon's tone had grown somber, a slight frown creasing her smooth brow. "You really *aren't* a kid anymore. This isn't the fifth grade with you and Caffey rolling around on the school ground."

"You kill me, little sister."

"I'm two years older than you, remember?" At nineteen, Sharon was still in that fleeting span of time when she wanted to look older than her years. "And what do you mean by 'I kill you,' anyway?"

Cassidy's eyes held a merry light. "One minute you're a sit-down comic, and the next you're my mother confessor, trying to get me to change my fractious ways."

"Putting Barbay in the hospital is a bit more than fractious, Cass. I believe *criminal* is the word you're looking for." Sharon watched the smile slip off her brother's face.

"How did you find out about that?"

"Everybody in town under the age of twenty knows about the legendary Warren Barbay getting whipped by a skinny kid named Cassidy Temple."

As usual Cassidy leaped to the offensive. "Yeah, well he had it comin'."

"And you've been duly appointed Knight Templar of Baton Rouge." Sharon tapped her brother on each shoulder with an imaginary sword. "Sir Cassidy of Istrouma, defender of the holy shrine of adolescent egos."

"That's not funny!"

"No, it isn't . . . and neither is using brass knuckles on somebody's face."

"Is there anything you don't know about me? How'd you find out about that?"

"You left them out on your bed a few months ago. You did an awful thing, Cass."

"It was the only way I could beat him."

"Whatever it takes," Sharon said, shaking her head

slowly back and forth. "Is that pretty much your philosophy?"

Cassidy ran his hand through his hair, pushing it back from his face. "Yeah, I guess so . . . sometimes, anyway. *Always* with somebody like Barbay."

Sharon got up and sat down on the bed next to her brother. "Cass, the only reason you're not in jail is because Barbay's got such a long rap sheet with the police they just kind of looked the other way this time. I guess they figured he finally got what he had coming for a long time."

"See," Cassidy's face brightened, "even the cops are on my side now."

"Next time you might not be so fortunate."

"Ah, c'mon, sis, give me a break, will you? I bet Austin ain't complainin'."

"Austin could have gone after Barbay and whipped him fair and square, Cassidy. Everybody in town, especially Barbay, knew Austin had him whipped except for that one lucky punch. And next time it wouldn't have happened. Austin would have beat him senseless . . . without using any weapon like you did."

"But he never did."

"That's right. . . . He never did."

"I wonder why. . . ."

Sharon leaned over and kissed Cassidy on the cheek. "When you find that out for yourself, little brother, you'll be on the way to becoming a man."

"What are you talkin' about?" Cassidy jumped off the bed, an incredulous look on his face. "I'm a man right now!"

Sharon responded to her brother's histrionics with a sweet smile, feeling his anger.

"You don't think so? Just go on down to the hospital and ask Barbay. He'll tell you."

"Barbay. . . . Is he your idea of a real man, Cass . . . or maybe just the resident expert on manhood?"

Cassidy opened his mouth but found that Sharon had boxed him into a corner. "Ah . . . what do you know about anything, anyway? You're just a girl." Getting no response, he whirled around and stormed out of the bedroom.

★ ★ ★

The woods stood cold, starkly barren at the approach of Thanksgiving. Leafless branches of the red oak, sycamore, and tupelo formed dark, intricate latticework against the iron gray cloud banks moving in from the northwest. On the forest floor lay leaf mold and decaying limbs, and palmetto stood scattered about in stiff, fanlike profusion. Far off in the distance, the harsh cawing of a single crow sounded like an anthem for the forests, lakes, bayous, and quiet backwaters of the trackless Atchafalaya Basin.

Cassidy, wearing combat boots, olive drab fatigue pants, and his father's marine field jacket from the Korean War, sat at the base of an ancient live oak, leaning back against its rough bark. He let his eyes take in the maze of limbs above and in front of him, waiting for that telltale twitching of burnt red color. Then off to his left, a fox squirrel, looking like a knot as it bunched against the side of a towering beech, signaled to one of its own kind with that cobra-quick flicking of its tail. Two minutes later it started a brief and final journey through its native pathways.

Cassidy lifted the Remington's heavy wood stock to his shoulder. Because he soon found the shots too easy to make, he had quit using a shotgun years ago in favor of his .22 automatic. As the squirrel began his graceful, erratic tracking through the trees, skittering along one limb and sailing out in space to another in a neighboring tree, Cassidy found the little creature's quick, hard body with the front bead sight, lining it up for windage and elevation with the open rear sight, waited for the squirrel's leap into open space, squeezed the trigger, and shot him out of the air.

As always with the hunt, time had seemed to slow to a crawl. The leap had been graceful, lovely, and a slow motion sailing against the sky's scudding gray clouds until the little .22 slug thumped into the squirrel's body just behind the foreleg, sending it tumbling down, down, down to the leafy floor of the forest a hundred feet below.

Too easy. No sport left in it. Ever since Cassidy had begun hunting, the rifle had always seemed more an extension of his arm than a weapon, almost as though the wild game he hunted simply fell lifeless when he pointed at them.

"Well, that's supper for three." Cassidy stood up and walked over to the spot where the squirrel lay in the deep red stillness of death. Picking it up, he stuffed it into his hunting sack and walked toward the lake. There, tucked away in the reeds and cattails, swaying in the wind, a pirogue rocked slowly in the waves, pushing against its shallow wooden sides.

Cassidy stepped into the fragile little craft and pushed his way out of the shallows with a short paddle. In the open water he stroked through the waves slapping against the pirogue's bow, throwing a cold spray into his face. Crossing the lake, he kept his eyes on the cabin built of rough-cut logs and resting on pilings seven feet above the shallows and forty feet out from the shoreline. In the failing lead-colored light of late afternoon, the warm glow of a lantern in the windows beckoned to him like the welcoming smile of an old friend.

As he paddled through the rough water, Cassidy let his mind wander back over the years, savoring the good times he had enjoyed with his family in this enclave of peace nestled deep within the Basin. A few minutes later, he saw his father walk down the steps from the front gallery to the dock.

"We heard six shots, Cass. Your reputation's down the drain if you don't have six squirrels tucked away in that hunting bag of yours." At forty-six, Lane Temple weighed five pounds more than when he played first-string quarterback for the Rebels of Ole Miss. Streaks of gray ran through his brown hair, but his chiseled features and jutting chin were as strong as ever and his brown eyes held a youthful light.

"Anything less than six, I'm not cleaning 'em." Dalton, Cassidy's older brother and a twenty-five-year-younger version of his father, opened the cabin door and stepped out onto the gallery. At six one, he looked the part of the all-American halfback he had been at LSU until a knee injury had blown away his dreams of a career in the pros.

Cassidy lifted the paddle out of the water, lay it across his legs, and let the pirogue glide alongside the dock, bumping gently against the tires that hung from the pilings. "I'll let you count 'em for yourself, Hero." He had coined the nickname for his brother during his glory days on the nation's premier playing fields, and the name had stayed on even after the thundering cheers in the stadiums had died away forever. "That is if you learned to count that high in that phys ed department out at LSU."

"Anytime you want to compare grades, you just let me know, little brother."

★ ★ ★

"You think Billy's gonna win the Heisman Trophy, Daddy?" Cassidy sat on the floor of the gallery, his back against the rough cypress planking of the wall. Using a hunk of French bread, he sopped up the last of the gravy from the squirrel stew Lane had prepared.

Lane, wearing the old World War II field jacket that had been issued after the signing of the peace treaty on the battleship *Missouri* in Tokyo Bay, chewed thoughtfully, swallowed, and said, "Yep . . . and Johnny Vaught is the man who's already won it for him."

"Vaught . . ." Dalton, wearing threadbare jeans and a heavy khaki shirt, sat on the gallery floor, his feet planted on the second step leading down to the dock. "How's the Ole Miss coach gonna win the Heisman for an LSU player?"

"Remember, he tried to sit on a three-point lead in the game this year," Lane explained. "You can't do that with an explosive runner like Cannon on the other team."

"Yeah," Dalton nodded, "I see what you mean. That one punt return on Halloween night is probably enough to cinch the Heisman . . . not to mention Billy's other three years as the best back in the country."

"You hung right in there with him, for those first two years until . . ." Lane regretted the words as soon as he had spoken them, but it was too late to call them back.

"You know something, Daddy?" Cassidy grinned at Dalton, deliberately changing the subject away from football. He looked down at his empty plate, then set it on the floor beside him. "That's *not* the best squirrel stew I ever ate."

Lane smiled at his youngest and most unpredictable child. "Thanks a lot, Cass. I can always count on you for a word of encouragement."

"I think it's pretty good, Daddy." Dalton's eyes still carried the shadows of past sorrow, surfaced by the mention of his fellow running back at LSU. "Better than you can do, Cass."

"Don't get me wrong," Cass said, holding his hands up, palms turned out toward Lane. "You're a great daddy . . . you just can't cook—that's all." He turned his cheshire grin on his father. "Looks like you're gettin' a little old and flabby, too."

Suddenly Lane whirled around out of his chair, grabbed Cass by the collar of his jacket and the seat of his pants, and held him over the edge of the porch. Cassidy squawked and flailed his arms, but to no avail.

"Who's old and flabby now?"

Cassidy glanced down at the dark surface of the lake almost ten feet below him. Cypress knees rose from the water like huge brown stalagmites. He relaxed, giving up the fight. "Maybe I was a little hasty in my judgment."

"And . . ." Lane kept his grip firm.

"And you're in great shape. I must have been looking at Dalton instead of you."

Lane dumped Cassidy on the gallery floor, then turned toward his oldest son. "Dalton, you gonna let this little twerp talk about you like that?"

Dalton had already gotten to his feet, legs flexed, arms spread in front of him in a wrestling posture. "I'm ready anytime you are, Cass."

Cassidy glanced around, knowing that Dalton's

weight and the strength gained from years of weight training for football were more than enough to handle him in the confined space of gallery and dock where his speed and cat-quick reflexes would do him little good. "I may have to take a rain check, Dalton. Daddy won't let me use my best tactic."

"Yeah, what's that?"

"Fighting dirty."

Lane laughed and sat back down in his chair, enjoying the company of his two very different sons. One as settled and solid as the heart cypress pilings of the cabin, the other as wild and unpredictable as an Oklahoma twister. "Well, it's been a good three days, boys," he said, listening to the wind-driven waves lapping against the dock, "but tomorrow we have to get up early so we can make it home in time for Thanksgiving dinner."

"Yeah, I don't want to miss out on any of that."

"What's Justine fixin'?" Cassidy asked, remembering the good meals Dalton's wife had prepared for them.

"A sweet potato casserole with that crusty pecan topping." Dalton moaned in anticipation. "Man, do I love that. She's bringing some other stuff, but that's all I remember."

"I never did figure out how 'Uncle Earl' got out of the nuthouse at Mandeville so fast." As usual, Cassidy blurted out whatever popped into his head. "How'd he manage that, Daddy?"

"It was a complicated business, son . . . even for Louisiana politics." Lane tilted his chair back against the wall of the cabin. "The way I heard it, the governor fired Jessie Bankston, who was the director of the Department of Institutions. Then he put his own man in to head it up."

Dalton stepped just inside the cabin door and turned on the battery-operated radio. Standing in the doorway he asked, "You mean he fired somebody while he was committed to the insane asylum?"

"That's what I heard," Lane continued, clasping his hands behind his head. "Then somehow Jack Gremillion, the state attorney general, and Joe Arthur Simms, the district attorney over in Covington, got together and filed a writ of habeas corpus in the twenty-second Judicial District Court, and the judge ordered our politically brilliant, but somewhat uncouth, governor Earl Long released."

"What a mess this state is," Dalton said, his voice freighted with contempt.

"Colorful," Cassidy corrected him. "What other state in this country would elect a lunatic one term and a Hollywood movie star the next?"

Dalton ignored Cassidy's puerile comments. "Daddy, I think sometimes you're the only man in the state legislature that's got any sense."

"That's not true, son. It's just that those of us who aren't so . . . *colorful* never make the headlines."

Its tube warmed up now, the radio burst forth with a Buddy Holly favorite:

Well, that'll be the day . . .

"Man, could that guy sing!" Cassidy turned toward the sound pouring out of the cabin door. "I sure hated it when he got killed in that plane crash."

"Ritchie Valens wasn't bad either," Dalton added.

"He was all right, but 'Oh Donna' just ain't in the same class with 'Raining in My Heart' or 'True Love Ways.' "

"I guess you're right at that," Dalton conceded, a rare happenstance between the brothers.

Lane and his sons sat on the gallery of the little

cypress cabin deep in the heart of the Atchafalaya wilderness. The rain began, slowly at first, the big drops pecking at the tin roof like tossed stones. Then it began in earnest, a wall of water marching across the flat expanse of lake from the northwest, the wind behind it blowing a cold spray across the length of the gallery, driving them inside the cabin.

"Might as well turn in early," Lane said, rolling the heavy wool army blanket back on his cot.

"I'm about done in anyway." Dalton yawned and climbed into the bottom bunk.

Cassidy shed his jacket and shoes, then leaped up onto the top bunk. He slipped down between the blanket and cool sheets, stretching lazily. The chill November rain soon slowed to a steady drumming on the roof, lulling him down, down into a soft, dark cloud of sleep. Later, as the rain slackened, a heavy fog moved across the surface of the lake, wrapping its cold white tendrils around the bases of the cypress, curling around the pilings of the dock and rising to enfold the steps, the gallery, and finally the entire cabin up to its windowsills.

THREE

BREAKING THE TAPE

★ ★ ★

Cassidy never looked down the length of parallel white lines tapering off into the distance against the gray cinders until they merged in his sight at the one-hundred-yard mark. He knew now by instinct exactly how far it was to the tape and the expenditure of lung and muscle power that it would cost him to break it.

For the past three months he had worked harder than he ever had in his life, laying off Cokes and sweets and giving up cigarettes completely. He had won all the preliminary events easily, never fully extending himself, waiting for the state meet to bring all the hard work and sacrifice and conditioning together in one final race. For the first time in his life he would know precisely what natural talent and hard work could accomplish in one supreme effort.

"Take your marks!" The man in red shorts and white shirt held the starter's pistol at shoulder level as he prepared to fire it in the final heat of the state championship's one-hundred-yard dash.

Cassidy approached the blocks, squatted down, and placed his fingertips and thumbs carefully on the chalk line. He set his left foot in the front block, kicked his right leg behind him in a final stretching exercise, and placed his right foot in the rear block. Taking a deep breath, he let his neck relax, staring down at the cinder track. But he saw nothing, his mind already beginning to flow with the controlled grace and power of the race ahead of him.

"Set!"

A final slow intake of breath, Cassidy's muscles bunched toward that vital explosion out of the blocks. Countless races had given him a feel for the timing of the starter's gun. A mere fraction of a second before his mind registered the pistol blast, Cassidy drove his right foot against the rear block with all the power of his calf and thigh and hip muscles unleashed in an instant of time.

Bang!

Cassidy's left leg uncoiled almost simultaneously, giving him a half-step lead out of the blocks. He straightened toward an upright, forward-leaning position as he picked up speed, his arms pumping in time with the smooth, powerful deer-quick strides of his legs. Wind whistled past his ears, blood coursing hotly through his veins and arteries, feeding oxygen to his straining muscles.

Unaware of anyone else on the track, Cassidy saw only the tape, red and taut and shining dully in the late, slanting southern sunlight. The finish line rushed at him, everything around him blurred to a gray nothingness, only the tape existed as he thrust his body forward with one final explosive burst of power, feeling the tape break like a quick, exquisite caress across his chest.

Then the total release of all pressure—all the leg-driving, lung-bursting, gut-wrenching burden of the race. He let the momentum of his flying body carry him on down the track, gradually slowing to a trot. Turning around, he walked back toward the men standing at the finish line, staring wide-eyed and some openmouthed at their stopwatches.

"This must be wrong," one of the men said.

The others crowded around in a ragged circle.

"Same time I got."

"Me too."

"Somebody get that starter down here."

Cassidy walked alongside his arch rival, a short, stocky, red-haired, coiled-spring of a kid from Fairpark High in Shreveport. For three years Cassidy had edged him out every time they had competed in a meet.

"I ain't never been beat so bad in my life."

Cassidy grinned. "Maybe you're gettin' old."

"Nah." He shook his head. "I don't know what you ran today, but whatever it was it's going down in the record books. That much I can tell you for sure."

"Think so?" Cassidy recalled the finish of the race. As usual he had glanced about after breaking the tape. No one had been anywhere near him.

"Hey, Cass. Great race!"

Cassidy watched Caffey lumbering toward him from the shot put area, where he had finished competing. "How'd you do?"

Caffey slowed to a walk. His arms and shoulders bulged in the skinny-strapped shirt, and the shiny red material of his shorts stretched tightly across his big thighs. "Third place. I never could get my form down today."

"You never listened to coach. That's your problem." Cassidy put his arm around his big friend's shoulder as they walked along. "You can't just arm that twelve-pound shot. You gotta get your shoulders and legs and body turned into it. Speed and form are just as important as strength."

Caffey shrugged, gazing down at the ground as they walked toward the Istrouma area where their gear lay on the ground. "I don't think I did good enough to get a scholarship, Cass. That's the only way I can afford to go to college."

"Tell you what, partner. You and me are gonna work on your form this summer, and by fall you'll be throwing that iron ball out of the stadium."

"You really think so?"

"Guaranteed."

As they sat down in their school area, slipping into their sweat jackets, the speakers on the public address system squawked shrilly. "Ladies and gentlemen," the announcer began, "we have the results in the finals of the one-hundred-yard dash."

Cassidy glanced toward the stands. His mother sat three rows up, wearing a pale blue dress and an expression of rapt attention to the words blaring out of the speakers.

Hurshell Mears—dark-haired, rugged, a construction worker during the summer—stood at the microphone. It seemed appropriate that he should make the announcement, as he had coached Cassidy all three high school years. "In first place is Cassidy Temple of Istrouma High School." The speakers squealed loudly, then returned to a dull hum. "And this young man from Baton Rouge has just set a new meet and state record of nine-point-six seconds!"

Cassidy heard a loud noise, part bull ape bellow and part Indian war cry, then felt a hard jarring slap on his back that sent him stumbling. "You trying to kill me, Caffey?"

Overcome with joy, Caffey picked his friend up on his shoulder as though he were a child, carrying him across the infield toward Catherine, who was now stepping carefully down the bleachers, her bright smile turned on her son sitting on the shoulder of his huge and happy friend.

Catherine met them at the gate leading out onto the track. "I'm so proud of you, Cass!"

"Will you put me down, you big ox?" Cassidy glanced at the people sitting in the bleachers closest to them, laughing at the stick of a boy carried on the shoulder of the wild-haired, gap-toothed, grinning giant.

Caffey let Cassidy slide down off his shoulder, holding him safely with one giant paw. "I'm real glad, Cass. You can go to any college you want now."

"If only Lane could have been here to see you." Catherine took her son by the shoulder, kissing him lightly on the cheek. "If there'd been any way for him to get out of that legislative session, you know he would have."

Cassidy smiled in the pure joy of the moment of his greatest victory. "Don't you think I know that, Mama? He's been my biggest fan ever since I started running track . . . except maybe for you. Besides, he'll have all those years to see me run with the best in the country when I'm at LSU."

Catherine stepped over to the bleachers, sitting down next to her son as Caffey plopped down opposite her. "You've decided, then. You're going to LSU."

"Yep. I don't think there was ever much doubt about it anyway. I've been in Baton Rouge since I was four." He gazed out at the runners, preparing for the next race. "Might as well stick around awhile longer."

★ ★ ★

Graduation night, May 27, 1960. The long line of jubilant cap-and-gowners stretched beneath the portico running from the rear of the gym past the band room and the cafeteria on to the main two-story school building. Imagine yourself walking along that concrete pathway leading to that graduation ceremony, to the freedom and the work and the terrors that awaited them out in the world of men and women. You would have youthful joy and excitement and ignorance spilling out of them into the mild, faintly jasmine-scented air.

"Finally . . . gettin' out of prison!"

"No more math exams."

"Or English themes to write."

"No homework."

"And no more crummy school lunches."

"I'm gonna sleep till noon every day."

"Free at last."

"I don't think it's so bad." For the eleventh time Caffey adjusted the mortarboard balanced on top of his big head, his wiry red hair pushing out from beneath it.

Cassidy pulled at the baggy sleeves of his pleated black gown. "What's not so bad?"

"School."

"Are you crazy?"

"Maybe, but it's still not a bad place." Caffey smiled his wide, placid smile. "I kinda like it here."

"What's the matter with you? You like all these rules?" Cassidy gestured wildly with his hands, his sleeves flopping about, exaggerating each point. "You like sittin' in a dumb chemistry class when we could

50

be out at the beach? You like some big dumb ex-jock walloping your backside with a board because you don't have a stupid corridor pass?"

"It wasn't so bad."

Cassidy shook his head slowly back and forth. "I don't know about you, Caffey. Sometimes I think your ol' man belted you in the head with that big fist one time too many."

"He did." Caffey stared out across the darkened school ground toward the invisible industrial arts building. "But I still like it here. Out there in the 'bullpen' we could sit around with the other guys and tell jokes and just act crazy . . . and smoke even."

"You quit smoking two years ago."

"Yeah, but it was still fun just to watch . . . just to hang around with the guys."

"You can still hang around with everybody when you get out of this jail."

"Won't be the same." Caffey shifted his vision farther out into the darkness toward the baseball diamond and the track. "I liked throwing the shot put . . . and you could hear the cheers from the bleachers and from over at the baseball field, too, and you didn't know whether they were for somebody running or throwing good, or whether somebody else might have hit a home run." His smile grew wider. "I just like it . . . that's all."

Cassidy put his hand on Caffey's rough jaw, turning his head around to face him. "You been drinkin' that cheap wine again, Caffey?"

Caffey shook his head.

"We're still gonna have fun when we get out of this nursery school, Caffey. You act like the world's comin' to an end." Cassidy thumped him on the shoulder with his fist. "And you're gonna be throwing the shot put out at LSU. We're gonna work hard this summer, and you'll be ready next year."

"You know what else I liked?"

"Oh no!" Cassidy placed his palm against his forehead. "Here we go again."

"I liked the trips in the school bus."

"You *liked* that ratty ol' bus?"

Caffey nodded, his expression serene as a cloistered nun's. "Especially ridin' home at night from a track meet over in Lake Charles or down at Jesuit. All the guys would be cuttin' up." He grinned at Cassidy and added, "You know like y'all always did."

"Yeah." Cassidy took a brief glance into the past but refused to dwell on it. He somehow knew, although the words never formed themselves in his mind, that it had been too perfect and too fragile to last. "I know."

"I guess maybe it was so much fun," Caffey stared off into the darkness again, "because I didn't have to be at home . . . didn't have to listen to Da—I mean my ol' man's ranting and raving about how I was stupid and wouldn't never amount to nothin'."

"Don't think about that, boy," Cassidy said, punching him playfully in the stomach. "This is a night for fun."

"Uh-huh. And you know what else I like?"

Cassidy merely shrugged, knowing Caffey was on a roll and wouldn't stop until he got everything off his mind.

"I like to hear Brother Dean pray."

"You mean Hershel's daddy?"

"Uh-huh."

"What's that got to do with anything?"

"It's on the program. He's gonna do the incova . . . I mean the invitation. No, that's not it either."

"Invocation, Caffey. The word is *invocation*."

"Yeah, that's it. It makes me feel good to hear him when he prays. I go to his church services sometimes, too."

"I'm happy for you." Cassidy rolled his eyes. "But after the invocation we're gonna dance and drink and have the best time we ever had in our lives. Whaddya say?"

Caffey nodded. "Okay." Then the smile slipped away. "But nothin's ever gonna be this good again."

"Yes, it will, son." Coach Mears laid his hand on Caffey's shoulder. "It's sad now because a part of your life is ending. That's just natural." He looked up into Caffey's big docile face. "I think maybe you're one of the few kids standing here in this long line with sense enough to know just how important"—he seemed almost hesitant with the next words—"how precious these days really are."

Cassidy steered the conversation away from sentiment. "You gonna help us get Caffey a track scholarship, Coach?"

Mears glanced at Cassidy, then turned his stern gaze on Caffey. "All track's been for you is just another place to hang around with Cassidy. Am I right?"

"Yes, sir."

"You willing to really work at it now?"

"Yes, sir."

"You never trained for your event, Caffey. I think you could throw the sixteen-pound college shot put close to sixty feet if you really worked at it."

"I'll do it, Coach. I wanna go to college with Cassidy. I'll work as hard as a mule to do that."

"You need to learn the discus, too. I know you never liked it, but they'll want you to do more than throw the shot put." He tapped his chin thoughtfully with the tip of his forefinger. "Speed, form, and timing . . . that's what it's going to take."

"I can do it, Coach. I got a reason now."

"All right. I'm working construction again all summer, but I get off at three-thirty. We'll get together here at the track Monday, Tuesday, and Thursday."

"Thanks, Coach. I'll work harder than anybody you ever saw. . . . I promise."

Mears smiled and took Caffey's extended hand. "I know you will." He then shook hands with Cassidy. "It's been a pleasure coaching you boys." Glancing around, he continued. "In fact, it's been fun coaching all my boys. Congratulations to both of you."

"Thanks, Coach." Cassidy watched the coach walk along the line, shaking hands, smiling, bidding farewell to the young people who had been a part of his life for three years. "Did you see that?"

"See what?" Caffey still had his eyes on the man who was going to help him get a scholarship.

"Tears. He had tears in his eyes."

"Coach?"

"Yep."

"I didn't see nothin'."

"Not just now. Earlier . . . after he got everybody lined up, when he was walking along looking at us."

"Coach? No kiddin'."

"No kiddin'."

★ ★ ★

The folding chairs had been picked up and stored away by the maintenance crew and the bleachers folded back against the wall. The graduation speeches had become a part of the dusty, unremembered history of Istrouma's senior classes stretching back through the years. What *would* be remembered was yet to come—the night-long celebration beginning with the senior prom and its whispered promises on the dance floor . . . and afterward. Unlike the speeches, these would be remembered . . . but probably not for very long.

Slim Harpo and his band opened the dance with the song that *he* would be remembered for:

Rainin' in my heart, since we been apart . . .

"Oh, I just love that song! C'mon, Cass." Kay, her white strapless gown shimmering in the dimmed overhead lights, pulled him out onto the dance floor.

Cassidy slipped his right arm around her slim waist, threading them through the massed couples who were gliding and turning across the slick, glossy hardwood floor laid out and marked for basketball. As they danced, Kay pressed against him, her eyes closed, her cheek resting against his starched tuxedo shirt.

But Cassidy gazed at the sea of faces moving past, flooding him with memories of his twelve years of school with these same classmates, suddenly grown old: a girl from the third grade whose name he could no longer remember had slapped him for pulling her pigtails; another, her mouth not quite as soft looking now, had kissed him when he was thirteen during his first game of "spin the bottle"; that boy, he was the one who had told the principal on him when he smoked his first cigarette in the boys' bathroom.

"Penny for your thoughts."

Cassidy gazed into Kay's upturned face. "Just thinking how lovely you are, sweetheart."

"I'll bet." Kay knew Cassidy's talent for saying whatever pleased her, but it sounded good anyway. "What's really on your mind?"

"All these years—all these sad and lovely golden

years—friends and strangers growing old in a single night." Cassidy gestured theatrically with his left hand as he spoke. "Friends and strangers pushing off in our fragile, blood-powered crafts on that dark and solitary journey." His impromptu speech finished, he grinned, slightly embarrassed by the words spoken on impulse. "Sounds good, don't it? Maybe someday I'll write a poem about this night."

"I think you just did." The song ended and Kay took Cassidy's arm as they left the dance floor. Harpo began his own version of Jimmy Clanton's only big hit.

Just a dream, just a dream; all our plans . . .

"Cass, we've just *got* to dance again. That's our song." Kay led him back out among the gliding couples. "Remember, we heard it on the radio on our first date. We were going to see *Ben-Hur* down at the Paramount."

"Yeah." It seemed to Cassidy that every other song he heard was "our song" to somebody he happened to be with at the time. He seldom remembered how the song had come to be "our song" but found it expedient to pretend that he did. "Imagine a boy from Baton Rouge making the national charts," he said.

"Dale and Grace had the number one song in the country last year," Kay said, smiling at friends as they moved across the floor. "Dale graduated two years ahead of us. I think Grace was from down in Ascension Parish."

Cassidy nodded, remembering "I'm Leavin' It All Up to You" as another of the "our songs" with someone else, although he couldn't put a face with it.

"All the boys look so handsome tonight." Kay touched Cassidy's black bow tie. "Don't you think so?"

"Ravishing," Cassidy said, glancing around the

dance floor. "Absolutely ravishing."

The song ended and they turned once again toward a cluster of friends gathered around a refreshment table.

Although his roots grew deep in black rhythm and blues, Harpo recognized the appeal of its Cajun and Creole counterpart, Swamp Pop. Its anthem, "Mathilda," was a particular favorite of his, and he could sing it with the best of the Cajun artists.

Mathilda, I cried and cried for you . . .

"Could we, Cass?" Kay gave him a pleading look. "Just this one more song."

Cassidy gazed at the cups of cold punch his friends were downing. "Why not?" He took Kay in his arms once again, felt her softly against him as they moved with the pulsing beat of the song.

Three hours later, Harpo's final number, "The Party's Over," ended the senior prom of 1960. The beginning of a new high school year would never come again for them. As the strains of song faded, a few moments of uneasy silence descended on the gym. Then the noise level suddenly increased as though everything left unspoken for the past twelve years must be said in these few remaining minutes.

Cassidy felt it then for the first time—an unexpected heavy aching in his chest, a longing for those days . . . and those friendships that were gone forever. The excitement of that first week of school; renewing old friendships and all the summer-bright and glowing girls showing off their new fall clothes; the pep rallies in the gym before the big game; the band thundering across the white-striped field in Memorial Stadium; after-school soda fountains with chocolate malts and jukebox tunes; parking in front of the house after dates and the winking summons of the front porch light; Friday-night parties and slow dancing to 45s played on a hi-fi record player; and the unexpected thrill of first loves and the unending sorrow of broken romances.

"It's kind of sad, isn't it?" Kay leaned against Cassidy, a tinge of weariness in her brown eyes.

"What?"

"Graduation, the last dance at the senior prom. I'm kind of happy, but I guess I'm mostly just sad."

"I think you're mostly just goofy. We finally escape this place and you're gettin' all teary eyed." Cassidy felt a thickness in his throat as he spoke.

Kay slipped her arms around his waist, resting her head against his chest. "I guess it's different with girls."

"Yeah."

FOUR

A Death in the Family

★ ★ ★

Cassidy eased the black '57 Chevy over to the side of the street, parking in front of Caffey's house. It stood next to his father's ramshackle mechanic shop that was no more than a single garage with a hand-painted sign tacked to the front. Scraps of tar paper, held in place by roofing tacks, clung to the walls of the unpainted clapboard shack. An ochre-colored tin roof helped shield a front porch whose sill had rotted on one end, causing it to slant almost down to the bare earth. A jagged chunk of concrete held what was left of it in place. In the alley between the house and the garage an ancient Plymouth coupe rusted into the weeds.

"I think these tuxedos might look a little funny in my house." Caffey grinned sheepishly, loosening his black bow tie and unbuttoning the stiff collar.

"Nah, we'll just be making some kind of new fashion statement." Cassidy opened the door to get out. "Who knows, it might catch on. We'll call it 'Elegance

Comes to Squalorville.' Those Fifth Avenue fashion salons will eat it up."

Caffey gazed at his friend with a blank expression. "Half the time I don't have no idea what you talkin' about." He laughed softly. "It sounds funny, anyway."

The two young men at the weary end of their graduation and prom night walked across the hardpan yard past Caffey's father, who was lying supine and ponderous in the front porch swing. He resembled an older, coarser, heavier version of Caffey that someone had smeared liberally with grease. Empty Dixie beer bottles and Picayune cigarette butts littered the floor beneath him.

Cassidy glanced at him as they walked by, then whispered to Caffey, "He looks like a big sack of feed that somebody put some clothes on."

Caffey, trudging around the side of the house, ignored his father as well as the comment. The weeds in back had grown almost as tall as the eaves, except for the narrow path Caffey had made over the years avoiding his father on the front porch. Car parts, an assortment of old tools, and trash littered an open area around the back door.

Carefully opening a screen door that hung drunkenly by one hinge, Caffey stepped on a grease-caked concrete block and up into the kitchen. Cassidy followed him inside. In the dim yellow gloom of a single forty-watt bulb screwed into a globeless fixture, he gazed about at the crusts of moldy bread, crushed Kellogg's Sugar Frosted Flakes boxes, Holsum Bread wrappers, chicken bones, and scraps of food lying about on the table, cabinet, and floor.

"Home sweet home," Caffey said, his voice dull and hollow sounding.

"Whew!" Cassidy expelled his breath in a rush. "I

can take this place in the wintertime, but not after it gets warm. See if you can find a bottle, and let's go outside."

Caffey opened the cabinet on the far left against the back wall, reached up, pushing a square Saltine cracker tin aside, and produced a bottle of Ten-High straight bourbon. With a triumphant smile, he turned around and held it toward Cassidy. "Look, almost half a bottle."

Cassidy took the bottle and made a face at it. "A renegade Comanche wouldn't drink this stuff."

Caffey glanced nervously through the front room toward his father, a dim, slumped figure through the screen door. "You and me would, though."

"You bet we would." Cassidy turned abruptly and walked over to the back door. Jumping down into the yard, he took three steps to his right and entered a tunnel-like path leading deep into the tall weeds.

A huge moon riding high and full in the black sky transformed the derelict backyard into a maze of deep shadow and silvery shimmering light. Slipping through a wire fence, its posts long rotted and held up only by a tangle of underbrush and saplings, Cassidy came out onto the bank of a canal. To his left, a shelter made of stakes hammered into the spongy ground and covered by two pieces of rusted, bent tin looked like something out of a Depression-era photograph. Four pallets of rough-cut planking served as the floor.

Cassidy walked over to the shelter and sat down on the floor facing the canal. Unscrewing the plastic top on the bottle, he took a sip. "Ughhh!" He shuddered and shook his head. "Gotta be a man to handle this stuff."

"Yeah," Caffey agreed, slouching down next to him. A bright slice of moonlight cut across his face.

He took a gulp from the bottle. "A crazy man."

Cassidy gazed down into the canal. Water gurgled around a half-submerged wringer-type washing machine. "Why'd we come out here, Caffey?"

Caffey's rough hands dwarfed the bottle they enclosed. "Beats me."

"You wanna know why I used to come to your house when we were kids?"

"Yeah."

"Danger."

Caffey shrugged, taking a sip out of the bottle and handing it to Cassidy.

"Anyway, I used to think it was dangerous." Cassidy grinned, his eyes crinkling at the corners. "Stealing your old man's cigarettes or a couple of his beers from the kitchen, thinking anytime he could wake up from a drunk and beat us up." He glanced at Caffey. "I used to pretend I was Jack, you know with the beanstalk, and your dad was the sleeping giant."

"If you'd ever seen him pitch one of his fits you woulda *known* it was dangerous."

"And back here it was like a jungle," Cassidy continued, his eyes taking on a luminous quality in the moonlight streaming through a gap in the roof. "Especially in the summertime. You could almost hear Tarzan yelling up in the treetops or Simba the lion roaring." He glanced at Caffey. "You remember what he called the elephant?"

Caffey shrugged.

"Tantor."

"That's nice to know." Caffey's bland face formed an expression of childlike contentment. "You remember the first time I met you?"

"Yeah." Cassidy gazed back through the years to the fifth grade at Istrouma Elementary. "First day of school, first fight of the year, first trip to the principal's office."

"You hit me with a book."

"What'd you expect?" Cassidy grabbed the bottle. "You were choking me to death."

"That's because you called me a flat-headed frog."

Cassidy laughed, remembering that warm September morning almost eight years before. "Yeah, I did call you that." He took a sip of bourbon. "It's been a lot of fun, partner."

"And a lot of fights."

"Same thing, ain't it?"

Caffey stared down into the canal. Moonlight shimmered on the water rippling around the old washing machine. "I guess you think it is."

"Ah, c'mon now, Caffey. You act like you never punched anybody's lights out."

"I didn't say that."

"What's the big deal, then?"

"I didn't think it was fun."

Cassidy punched him on the shoulder. "Not even when ol' Barbay finally got what he had comin' to him?"

"He's kinda bad off now, Cass."

"Good." Cassidy noticed the troubled expression on Caffey's face. "What do you mean, 'bad off'?"

Caffey glanced at him, then stared back at the canal. "His mind ain't right now."

"Are you kiddin' me?" Cassidy's voice rose in indignation. "His mind ain't *never* been right." He grabbed Caffey by the front of his shirt. "I guess you gonna blame that on me!"

The look in Caffey's mild, slightly glazed eyes answered for him as he turned to his friend.

Cassidy found that he couldn't hold Caffey's gaze.

"He started it. . . . I finished it." He rumpled Caffey's bristly hair. "C'mon, let's forget about it. We got a whole summer of fun in front of us before we start LSU."

"I gotta work on the shot put and discus."

"I know. Coach Mears is gonna have you goin' to the Olympics if you do what he says."

Caffey smiled, turning his sincere eyes on Cassidy. "I'm gonna work hard."

"I know you will, ol' buddy. We've been going to school together too long to end it now."

"Yeah. Good times ahead for us." Caffey slipped out from underneath the ragged pieces of tin and stood up. "I'm wore out. Let's go."

Cassidy followed him back down the path, feeling a sense of comfort at the sight of Caffey's huge bulk trudging along in front of him.

Caffey did not turn around until he stopped at the back door of the house. "Want a smoke before you go home?"

Cassidy nodded and followed him into the kitchen.

Reaching up into the cabinet for the cigarettes, Caffey bumped the cracker tin. It bounced off the cabinet and went clanging across the kitchen linoleum. "Oh no!" His face drained of color as he stared at the front porch. "I'm in for it now."

Both boys froze, waiting for the snorting, growling sound of Caffey's father waking up. For ten seconds they stood motionless, glancing out toward the porch and then at each other. No sound . . . no movement from the man in the swing.

Caffey took a deep breath, letting it out slowly. "Something's wrong. I gotta see." He walked carefully through the front room. The screen door creaked as he opened it.

Cassidy watched his friend, in the murky darkness of the front porch, reach over and shake his father; heard the plaintive, raspy sound of his words.

"Daddy . . . Daddy . . . Daddy . . ."

★ ★ ★

"What a time to start work," Cassidy muttered to himself as he walked south along Plank road. He shivered slightly in the predawn dampness. Taking the blue plaid shirt he had slung over his shoulder, he slipped it on over his white T-shirt and stuffed it into his Levi's. Above him the stars glittered in a moonless sky. An occasional car passed by, its headlights searching the almost empty streets and sidewalks. Down the street he saw the gravel parking lot and squat block building of Wayne's Bakery.

Crossing the parking lot, Cassidy glanced at the panel truck he would be driving, then entered through the side door into the neon glare and muted commotion of the bakery. Huge mixers beat the dough to the precise texture demanded by Charles Daquano, who had started the business back in 1945. Conveyer belts hummed along, carrying bread dough past an employee who dusted it with flour, then on to a rolling machine; steam boxes hardened the crust to perfection as the bread baked, but also added humidity to the already moisture-laden South Louisiana air.

Cassidy grinned as he inhaled deeply the aroma of freshly baked French bread, "Hopper's Loaves," used at the popular drive-in, "Little Edward's" rolls, muffulettas, as well as the sugary scent of the pastries.

"You look like you're ready to eat instead of work." Daquano, who had named the bakery for his young son, pushed a cart stacked with French bread wrapped in paper sleeves over near the door. His receding hairline said "middle age," but long hours and hard work had kept his body trim.

"The smell of this place always gives me an appetite." Cassidy took another deep breath.

"Let's have a little snack, then." Daquano glanced at the schoolhouse clock behind him. "I been at it since three. Time for a break." He grabbed a loaf of bread from one of the shelves on the cart, wiped his hands on a white apron, and walked over to the coffee service against the wall.

Cassidy glanced at the stacks of bread. "Guess I'd better load the truck and get on the road."

"You don't go on the clock till five. You still got fifteen minutes." Daquano poured coffee into two thick white mugs, added sugar to both, and stirred them.

Lifting the mug to his lips, Cassidy took a sip of the rich, dark coffee. "Hmm . . . nothing like that first swallow of coffee in the morning."

"This is better." Daquano slipped the bread out of its wrapper, then broke off a hunk and handed it to Cassidy.

Biting into the warm bread, crusty brown outside and chewy white inside, Cassidy nodded in agreement. "You're right . . . it is better," he mumbled.

"How's Caffey coming along with the shot put?"

Cassidy swallowed, then said, "Doin' great! Coach Mears says he's already talked to Coach Moreau out at LSU about giving him a tryout."

"Good. That poor boy deserves a break." A shadow troubled Daquano's warm brown eyes. "Gettin' left alone with his daddy dying like that."

"He's better off." Cassidy took another bite of bread and watched a short, dumpy lady with a flowered blouse enter the bright retail area at the front of the bakery and begin to set up the glass counters with fresh pastries.

"I know his daddy wasn't no jewel, but at least he had somebody to look out for him."

"Now he's got me," Cassidy said flatly. "His ol' man never gave him anything but the back of his hand . . . or the front of his fist." He sipped his coffee.

"How's he gettin' by?"

"Social security. He can get veteran's benefits to help pay for his college, too."

Daquano glanced at an older man in khakis and a John Deere cap pushing a metal cart of freshly baked cakes toward the front of the bakery. "That give him enough to make it?"

"Mr. Short gave him a job at his sports shop. He's putting a little money aside, and Coach says at the least LSU should give him a scholarship to pay tuition and books." Cassidy spoke above the sound of the cart clattering along the concrete floor. "He's already throwing over fifty feet."

"Good." Daquano sipped his coffee, his eyes missing little that was going on in the bakery. "Your father told me you already signed with the Tigers."

Cassidy nodded, his mouth full of bread.

"Sounds like you boys are all set. How d'ya like the baking business?"

"I like the delivery part of it so far . . . runnin' around town and meetin' all the people."

"They like you, too . . . always on time, friendly, and a good worker."

Giving Daquano an oblique glance, Cassidy said, "You been checkin' up on me?"

"That's how I stay in business, son. Got to stay on top of everything." Daquano called out across the shop, "Sprinkle just a bit more flour on there, son."

"They like me, huh?"

Daquano smiled. "Yep. That's what they tell me." His eyes stared back through the years. "My daddy was a baker. He taught me a lot, but I wanted to find out more about the science of the trade, so I went to study up at the Dunwoody Institute for bakers in Minnesota."

"We got the best food in the country right here in South Louisiana. How could them Yankees teach you anything?"

"The recipe I been using since I got back is from what I learned up there," Daquano explained. "It's based on a sponge, and I've kept it going all these years."

"What's a sponge?"

"Each day we save a little of the dough to serve as the starter for the next day's batch. It's called a sponge."

Cassidy swallowed the last of his bread. "Well, you make the best bread in town, even if you did learn it from the Yankees up in Minnesota." He headed toward the tall cart, its shelves loaded with bread.

"I'll get somebody to bring the rest of your load over." Daquano turned and walked toward the back of the building, stopping near one of the huge ovens. "Keep your eye on that temperature gauge."

★ ★ ★

An indecipherable black-and-white image formed in front of the audience. As the camera gradually pulled back, the object took the shape of an eye, open and staring blankly, filling the entire screen with its chilling message.

"That's an eye! It's *her* eye!" Kay stood up in the darkened theater. "Let's get out of here."

Cassidy slouched down in his seat with his legs draped over the back of the seat ahead of him, wrinkling the blue plaid shirt and chinos that Sharon had so neatly ironed for his date. "Ah, c'mon. It's just a movie."

"Yeah, Kay. A movie can't hurt you." Caffey sat in the end seat, his leg stretched out in the aisle.

Kay glanced at the screen. The eye had become the face of Janet Lee, resting against the white porcelain bottom of the bathtub. "No. I mean it." She shuddered. "First that awful stabbing scene and now this big eye. It's just too much!"

Cassidy groaned, dragging his legs off the seat back, then got to his feet. "C'mon, Caffey, we might as well go. She's actin' like a three-year-old again."

"I most certainly am not!" Kay straightened the waistband of her pale green skirt and slung her purse over her shoulder. "This is just too sick for anybody to see. As long as people keep watching these blood-and-gore movies, Hollywood will just keep turning them out."

"Spare us the lecture." Cassidy stood with his hands on his hips, waiting for Caffey to unfold himself from his seat. "Next time we'll go see *Goofy and Pluto Go to Sunday School*. Maybe that won't offend you."

Caffey snorted with laughter as he brushed the popcorn off his wrinkled work trousers.

"That's not funny," Kay snapped, slipping past the seats to the aisle. She pointed to the Don Short's Sporting Goods patch on Caffey's green twill shirt. "And does he have to be a walking billboard wherever we go?"

Cassidy held out his hands, joined at the thumbs, gazing between them at the shirt. "Caffey's making another fashion statement. He's always been ahead of his time."

Kay glanced at the shirt, then shook her head and started down the aisle toward the lighted exit door.

Cassidy followed closely after her. "No kiddin', Kay. You just watch. Dobie Gillis'll be wearing a Don Short's Sporting Goods patch on his next show."

In the bright lobby, its walls hung with posters of coming attractions, Kay watched Caffey head toward the concession stand, then turned to Cassidy. "Do you *always* have to bring Caffey along when we go out?"

Cassidy gazed at his friend, buying a box of Milk Duds. "He doesn't have any other friends, Kay." His smile faded, the blue eyes tinged with an undefined sadness. "Caffey just doesn't . . . fit in very well. You know he hardly ever got asked to parties and things like that. People just don't understand him. One look and they either laugh at him or they're scared to death." He brightened again as Caffey headed back toward them, lowering his voice. "And besides, I don't *always* bring him along."

"Anybody want a Milk Dud?" Caffey's docile smile spread across his broad face.

Kay shook her head, turned, and walked past the ticket booth and through the glass doors onto the sidewalk.

"Did I do something wrong?"

"Nah." Cassidy followed after her.

"What's wrong with Kay?"

"Who knows?" Cassidy grinned at Caffey lumbering along beside him. "Women . . ."

★ ★ ★

Hearing Cassidy climbing the stairs and walking

down the hall, Sharon stopped typing. "You're home early."

"This gettin' up at four in the morning is killing me." Cassidy stopped and leaned against the door-frame, gazing into the shadowy bedroom lit only by Sharon's desk lamp. "Did somebody chain you in front of that typewriter?"

Sharon laughed softly, sliding her chair around and propping her feet on the foot of her bed. She wore thick cotton socks, white shorts, and a T-shirt with *Istrouma Track* in red letters. "Sometimes I feel like that."

Cassidy stepped into the bedroom and sat down on the edge of the bed. "What happens when you finish the book?"

"Then I start looking for a publisher. I'll send out the manuscript and hope it lands on the right desk."

"The right desk?"

"Some editor who likes it enough to send it on up the line to whoever decides what books are published."

"You don't sound like you know very much about the publishing business."

"I don't," Sharon admitted, stretching lazily, "but I've got to start somewhere."

Cassidy lay across the bed, propped on one elbow. "Sharon, you're only twenty years old with two years of college behind you. What chance do you have of getting a novel published?" He lay back, clasping his hands behind his head.

"Not much. That's the hardest part of this business—sticking with it when the only thing you're getting back is a desk drawer full of rejection slips." Sharon's eyebrows raised a quarter inch. She spun around and typed for thirty seconds, then walked around and lay down on the bed, propping her feet on Cassidy's stomach.

"What was that all about?"

"It just suddenly hit me how to finish that scene." She closed her eyes, letting her breath out softly. "You don't talk much about Kay anymore."

"Who?"

"You know what I'm talking about. Are you two having problems?"

Lightning winked at the window; seconds later thunder growled lazily.

"*I'm* not. *She* seems to be . . . once in a while, anyway." Cassidy glanced at Sharon's desk, thinking of the months she had spent working on her novel while carrying a full load at LSU. "I think she wants to get married and have a family right away. That's the last thing on my mind."

White light suddenly flashed at the window, followed by the heavy rumbling of thunder. Wind rustled the leaves on the big oak outside the window and pushed the curtains against the side of the bed. The temperature in the room dropped five degrees.

"Sometimes I think there's a . . . restlessness about you, Cass, that won't ever let you settle down." Sharon pulled the corner of the chenille bedspread across her. "What do you want to take in college?"

"Don't know."

"How about English? Teaching maybe."

"You're kidding. What do I know about that?"

Sharon bumped him on the stomach with her heel. "This is me, Cass. Don't try to pull that stuff. I know you."

Cassidy stared at the ceiling.

"You've read everything in my library." Sharon heard the first drops of rain ticking in the leaves of the oak. "And I've seen enough of your English themes over the years to know that you've got a talent for writing."

"That's all I ever do, though," Cassidy said in a far-away voice. "Only what I have to."

"Not true," Sharon said. "You've worked as hard on your running as Dalton did on his football . . . and that's a lot of work. I've heard you go down those stairs at five in the morning on school days for too many years; seen you run down the driveway out to the street and come back an hour later dripping wet and half dead."

"Track's different."

"Work is work, Cass. Doesn't matter what kind—mental or physical—it all takes commitment and te-nacity. And you've got what it takes if you put your mind to it."

Cassidy dumped her feet aside and sat up in bed, crossing his legs and resting his elbows on his knees. "Gee, sis, I didn't know I was such a great guy till to-night." He spread his arms wide. "Maybe I could quit track and get a scholarship to LSU for just being so wonderful. If you'd go along as my agent, I think we could pull it off."

"I wonder how Kay's put up with you so long." Sharon hit him in the face with a pillow.

Cassidy rolled over laughing, holding his stomach. Then he sat up. "How could you even think of hitting somebody as wonderful as me?"

"Hey, don't you have to be at the bakery by five o'clock?"

"Ohhh . . . you would have to bring that up," he moaned. "I can't figure out why somebody who hates getting up in the morning as bad as I do ever took a job like this."

"Probably because it was the only offer you got."

Cassidy nodded in agreement. "That's it. I knew there had to be a good reason."

"Good night, Cass."

Cassidy got up to leave, then turned quickly and kissed his sister on the cheek.

An expression of mild shock on her face, Sharon asked, "What's that for?"

"I just feel especially benevolent tonight." He turned and headed toward the door, singing a parody of the Doris Day hit, "Mr. Wonderful . . . that's me."

PART TWO
★ ★ ★

TAKEN BY THE SEA

FIVE

COLLEGE LIFE

★ ★ ★

Wearing tan slacks and a navy button-down shirt, his hair still damp from his morning shower, Cassidy walked into the gym located next to the LSU Field House, took one look, and said, "I hate registration!"

"How could you hate it?" Caffey asked. "We just started." Sharon had ironed his tan chinos and pale yellow button-down oxford shirt in the hopes of giving him that neat Ivy League appearance. On Caffey, the clothes looked as though someone had tried to dress a small abandoned warehouse.

Cassidy stared at the long rows of folding tables, sprouting longer lines of babbling freshmen, stretched across the gleaming oak basketball floor. "Might as well get this over with." Spotting the placard marked S-Z, he walked toward the line of students waiting to get their schedule cards.

"English I-A, Physical Science . . ." Caffey looked up from the notes he had taken from the school catalogue. "You think we can find all these subjects,

Cass?" He shook his head. "This campus is a mighty big place."

"Don't worry about it. We'll find 'em." Cassidy stepped to the end of the line and flashed his best man-about-town smile at the girl ahead of him, taking a quick inventory. She had short dark hair, nicely revealing a slender, delicate neck. Long lashes shaded her dark brown eyes. No more than five-two, she wore a straight skirt in a checked pattern and a peach-colored blouse.

"Don't you just hate registration?" she asked.

Cassidy nodded toward Caffey. "I was just telling my friend here the very same thing."

"Oh . . ." The girl gazed up with some misgiving at Caffey's bulk only three feet away.

Noticing her expression, he said, "I'm Cassidy Temple and this is my oldest friend, Caffey Sams. Don't let his size fool you. He's just a big ol' teddy bear at heart."

The girl gave Cassidy an uncertain smile. "Ginger Clesi. Pleased to meet you both." She held out her slim hand, greeting them with some trepidation.

"Where you from, Ginger?" Cassidy shuffled alongside her in the slow-moving line.

Ginger glanced again at Caffey, who was studying his notes. "It's just a little place. You've probably never even heard of it."

"Try me."

"Bayou Ramah."

"Sure, I know where it is. My uncle Coley's from Grosse Tete just south of there." Cassidy found that he liked Ginger's easy smile and slow Cajun accent. "We go to his fishing camp down in the Basin all the time."

"You mean Coley Thibodeaux . . . the one who used to be a state representative?"

"That's him."

Ginger looked as though she had found a long-lost brother. "He's a cousin of mine from my mama's side of the family. Distant, but still kin."

"No kiddin'?"

Studying Cassidy's whitish blond hair and blue eyes, Ginger said, "He's your uncle? You don't look much like one of the Thibodeauxs to me."

"He's not a real uncle, but he's like one of the family. My dad and him have been best friends since we moved down here from Mississippi back in '46."

"Your daddy's Lane Temple, the one who took Coley's seat in the House."

"Yep. That's him."

"And you run track, don't you?" Ginger had become animated, punctuating her declarations with hand gestures and decorating them with subtle motions of her eyelashes. "My brother used to talk about how fast you were."

"Caffey's on the track team, too," Cassidy said magnanimously, patting his friend on the shoulder. "He's gonna beat Billy Cannon's shot put record, ain't you, Caffey?"

"I'm sure gonna try."

Mutual acquaintances and the obvious attraction of Cassidy and Ginger for each other quickly cemented the new friendships. The three of them were handed their schedule cards by an upperclassman with a stiff flattop haircut and an even stiffer resistance to any change in their assigned subjects. Resigned to their fate, they set out across the campus for Allen Hall to get their English class cards.

At both entrances to Allen Hall, a group of five or six upperclassmen waited with clippers and a makeshift barber's chair for any freshmen who didn't have the mandatory quarter-inch haircut.

"Hey, Whitey!" A stocky senior with black hair cut short, parted, and slicked to the sides of his narrow head, motioned to Cassidy. He wore a Sigma Chi T-shirt and held a pair of clippers in his right hand. "Get over here and have a seat. We got some styling to do on your locks."

"Frat rats," Cassidy whispered to Caffey. His eyes sparked, then he opened his mouth to tell the boy what he could do with his clippers when he felt a soft hand on his arm.

"Don't be ugly to him, Cassidy," Ginger pleaded with her words and her eyes. "I just can't stand harsh talk."

Glancing at "Clippers," Cassidy took a deep breath and exhaled loudly. "Neither can I."

Noticing Cassidy's hand crumpling into a fist, Ginger asked, "You're not the kind to get in fights, are you?"

Cassidy looked insulted and grieved at her words. "Why, no, indeed not. That's barbaric!" He forced an insidious smile on his face. "Look, why don't you just go on ahead and get your class card. We'll be there in a minute." Turning his smile on Clippers, he said, "This is just a little misunderstanding."

Ginger nodded, patted Cassidy on the arm, and walked down the hall, calling back over her shoulder, "Don't be long now."

The smile frozen on his face, Cassidy said sweetly, "Don't worry. We'll be right there."

The five young men had finally noticed Caffey's immense bulk and the biceps that threatened to split his shirt sleeves. They also appeared somewhat chagrined at the total lack of fear in his relaxed attitude. All five turned their attention on Cassidy with Clippers as the designated spokesman.

"C'mon, Whitey," he said through a big grin. "You might as well come on over here and get it over with. I think you'll find life a lot easier if you don't give us any trouble."

Cassidy glanced down the hall, noting that Ginger had disappeared into a classroom. His eyes suddenly drained of light, becoming cold and expressionless. "Anything comes easy ain't worth havin'."

Clippers grinned and looked at his buddies. "Five of us and one of you."

"Two of us." Caffey's voice rumbled above the noise in the crowded hallway.

"We ain't got no argument with you."

"That's right, Caffey. Why don't you go on with Ginger and get your class card."

"Ah, Cass."

"Go on. This won't take long."

Clippers couldn't believe his good fortune. "Yeah. You listen to your friend, big guy."

Suddenly a gleam of recognition registered on one of the faces at the table. He stepped over to Clippers, speaking in a low tone, but just loud enough for Cassidy to hear. "That's the guy put Barbay in the hospital."

"Him?" Clippers' face was draining of color. "You sure?"

"Positive," his friend said, backing off.

As Caffey ambled down the hall, Cassidy stepped directly in front of Clippers. Noticing movement to his left, he watched the last of the foursome disappear around the corner of the hall. "Looks like it's just you and me . . . Frat Rat."

His face ashen, he laid the clippers carefully down on the table and walked away as though he was coming into a house late at night, making almost no sound on the tiled floor of the hallway. A few interested passersby grinned or merely shrugged, then went about their business.

Cassidy saw Ginger step into the hallway and walk over to Caffey. As he strolled casually down the hall to join them, Cassidy saw the pained expression on her face.

"I thought those boys were going to start some trouble," Ginger said as Cassidy walked up.

"Nah," he glanced at Caffey. "I think they decided it wasn't worth it when Caffey stepped in."

Ginger smiled at her new friend, his wide, placid face as honest as an open Bible. "I'm glad you're Cassidy's friend." She took Cassidy's arm as they headed toward the room to get his class card. "You seem like such a pushover, I'm sure you need somebody like Caffey around to take care of you."

Caffey rolled his eyes toward the ceiling and fell in beside them.

★ ★ ★

"Okay. Somebody didn't put a name on this present." Cassidy, already wearing the new red sweater that Sharon had given him for Christmas, walked around the living room amid the clutter of paper and ribbons and toys, trying to hand out the last of the gifts. Behind him a tall spruce bubbled gaily with red and green and white lights that had been in the family since before he was born. A white-robed, golden-haloed shining angel that had belonged to Catherine's mother surveyed the family celebration from its vantage point at the top of the tree.

Catherine sat next to Lane on the big overstuffed

sofa. "That's *your* wrapping, Cass. I'd recognize it any-where."

Cassidy gazed down at the crinkled paper covered with leaping reindeer and held in place with masking tape. "Oh yeah, I remember. This is for you, Daddy."

Lane finished buttoning his new silver gray cardigan and reached for the gift. "Thanks, son. I hope you didn't dig too deep into your savings."

"You know me," Cassidy said, reaching for another present from under the tree. "I'm rollin' in money since I had that summer job at Wayne's Bakery." Just then something thudded into his legs from behind. Turning around, he gazed down at Taylor Young-blood, his sister Jessie's son, scratching for the present. "All right, rascal, you can help."

Taylor babbled excitedly as Cassidy picked him up. "Wanna help." The child had his father's black hair, but his bright blue eyes were a replica of Cassidy's.

Cass lifted his nephew in his arms and handed him the present. "This belongs to Aunt Justine. Let's go give it to her." He carried the child, beaming with delight, over to one of the big tapestry-patterned Queen Anne chairs, where Dalton sat opening a boxed gift the size of a bed pillow.

"Thank you, Taylor. You're a sweet boy." Justine, her reddish blond hair shining in the muted light from the tree, sat on the gleaming hardwood floor next to her husband. "Look, Dalton. It's for both of us from your mother and daddy."

Married six months now, Dalton gave her hand a husbandly squeeze. "You go ahead and open it, sweet-heart. I wanna see what's in this one."

The present delivered, Cassidy had started some-thing that he couldn't end so easily. Taylor pointed to the presents left beneath the tree, urging his uncle

Cassidy for more deliveries in the common language of two-year-olds. "More!"

"All right, you little wiggle worm, you can give the rest of them out. Here, this one goes to your aunt Sharon."

"Sha-won."

"Hold on a minute." Jessie, sitting near the tree next to Austin, dumped her partially opened present in his lap and crawled over to her son, her pale blond hair spilling across her face. "He's coming out of his new clothes." She adjusted and rebuttoned the blue overalls with a bright yellow Donald Duck on the bib while Taylor squirmed and fussed, eager to get back to his designated job of present delivery.

"I wonder if that could be a book." Aaron Walters, a halfback in high school and Sharon's steady boy-friend since they were sophomores, proved too small to play college ball, so he had thrown his abundant energies into getting an engineering degree at LSU. He glanced at the book-shaped gift, torn at one cor-ner, revealing part of a slick cover. "You did a fine wrapping job on this, Taylor. I'll bet your uncle Cas-sidy didn't even help you."

"I think it looks pretty good myself," Cassidy said, appraising his crinkled and torn Santa Claus paper as Taylor handed the gift over. Then he turned toward Aaron. "I saw your present to Sharon. It looked like it was wrapped by a drunk monkey wearing a blind-fold."

Catherine Temple held her cup of tea with both hands and curled up next to her husband on the sofa. Noticing the delicate grapevine pattern circling the rim, she remembered that this was one of only two cups left from a set she had received as a wedding present. She had managed to keep the number at three for years, then Taylor had come along and quickly reduced it to two.

She watched Jessie, her oldest, return to sit next to her husband. Austin had attended Harvard Law School and now had a new but thriving law practice downtown. She was grateful that Jessie, after her whirlwind years of trying to make it as a singer in Hollywood and Memphis, had settled down happily as wife, mother, and music teacher.

And Dalton, what a time you had after your football injury! But what Satan meant for evil, God turned to good. I couldn't have picked a better wife than the one He gave you during your self-imposed exile down in New Orleans. It's such a comfort having you and Justine living out back in the garage apartment. I know you'll be leaving in June when you graduate, but for now I'll just enjoy having both of you so near.

"Dalton . . ." Catherine suddenly remembered.

"Yes, ma'am." Dalton grinned at his mother, thinking that she had forgotten.

"Did you find out about the coaching job at LSU?"

Dalton obviously enjoyed keeping his mother in suspense. "Yes, ma'am, I did."

"Well . . ." Catherine leaned forward on the couch, eager for the news.

A slow smile crawled across Dalton's face. "Coach Dietzel said I can start this summer."

"Oh, that's wonderful!" Catherine placed her cup on the end table, then gave Lane a puzzled look. "Lane, aren't you excited about Dalton's job?"

Lane tore the last of the paper from his gift, then held the slim tan leather briefcase on his lap, popping the latches and opening the lid. "You must have seen that ragged ol' thing I've been packing around, Cass."

Cassidy held Taylor, who was shoving a present

into Sharon's outstretched hands. "Yeah. It looked like something you dug out of a Salvation Army box."

Lane beamed at his new briefcase. "This is just what I needed. Anything bigger than this just makes it too cumbersome."

Catherine gave Lane a puzzled look. "Aren't you excited about Dalton's job?"

"I already knew."

"You what? When did you find out?"

Inspecting the interior of his new briefcase, Lane said matter-of-factly, "I asked him hours ago when he walked through the kitchen door."

"And you didn't tell me?"

Lane grinned at Dalton, who was enjoying his mother's disbelief that they hadn't told her. "I figured if you were interested you'd ask him yourself."

Catherine grabbed her husband's ear, twisting it until he yelped. "Next time I'll let you and Dalton do all the cooking and see how much time you've got to ask questions."

Rubbing his ear, Lane called across the room, "Austin, I need a good lawyer over here. I've got a clear-cut case of physical anguish and suffering."

"Sorry, Dad." Austin, whose light gray eyes contrasted strikingly with his black hair, gave Catherine a quick smile. "I might not get a second helping of that special pecan pie my mother-in-law makes."

"See what a smart boy Jessie married?" Catherine slipped out of her shoes, lifting her stocking feet up on the couch. As she sipped her tea and gazed about the living room filled with her family enjoying Christmas together, her heart filled with gratitude.

Father, thank you for our family, for another Christmas together. May we never take for granted the miracle of children, of families sustained from generation to generation by your Word, your mercy, your grace.

★ ★ ★

Lane stretched out on the big sofa, a pillow beneath his head. "What a day!"

Catherine lay next to him, her head cradled against his shoulder. "A beautiful Christmas." She stared at the lights bubbling away on the tree.

"It's so good to have a baby in the house again! Next year he'll be old enough to get a football and shoulder pads, a helmet . . . the whole works."

"Maybe Dalton and Justine will have a girl." Catherine sighed deeply. "I'd sure love that."

"Do you know something I don't?"

"No, just wishful thinking."

Lane let his fingers trail through Catherine's hair. "Good. I'd just as soon see him get settled into his job before they have any children."

"Do you think Sharon and Aaron will get married?"

Lane listened to the big console radio playing softly as Elvis sang "I'll Be Home for Christmas." "I think she could do a lot worse than Aaron."

"That's not exactly high praise."

"You have to remember, Cath," Lane said, his voice growing drowsy. "Nobody's good enough for Sharon." He shifted his weight slightly on the couch. "Aaron's a good boy, though. He sure stuck by Sharon when she was so sick. And he's a hard worker. I have to give him that, too."

"I think he's good for her," Catherine sighed, Lane's drowsiness seeping into her. "Sharon's a dreamer, and Aaron's as practical and sensible as they come. I think they make a good pair."

"Taylor's a cutter, isn't he?"

"That he is," Catherine agreed. "I think that little boy's got a lot of his uncle Cass in him."

"I'll contact the juvenile probation department first thing Monday morning. They'll probably want to get a file opened on him early."

Catherine raised up on one elbow. "Lane Temple, you should be ashamed of yourself!"

Lane tried to stop the corners of his mouth from lifting in a grin. "Oh, I am. I'm purely mortified."

"You sound like a Mississippi redneck now."

"And proud of it." The tone of Lane's voice grew somber. "I'm concerned about him, Cath."

"Cassidy?"

"It keeps coming back to me . . . that fight he had with the Barbay boy."

"Boy? He was a twenty-six-year-old man when it happened. And *he* started it."

"Settle down, Cath." Lane enclosed her left hand with his right. "Cass's got such a good heart in some ways. Like with Caffey. If it wasn't for Cassidy, that poor boy would have probably grown up like a hermit. I've seen over the years how Cass was his friend when everybody else was either ashamed or afraid to be."

"Don't forget that he and Cass met because Cass was standing up for another boy that everybody else just made fun of."

"George Newsom." Lane let his mind drift backward, seeing again Cassidy's little friend with the glazed look about his brown eyes and the docile smile of acceptance that was his only defense against the teasing of other children . . . until he met Cassidy. "Another castaway that Cassidy took under his wing."

Catherine settled back down on the couch. "Well, why do you say such things about him, then?"

"Because I'm truly concerned, Cath." Lane gave

his wife's hand a reassuring squeeze. "I'm afraid this
. . . streak of violence in him is going to . . . if the cops
hadn't been so glad that somebody finally put Barbay
out of commission, Cassidy would probably have
served some jail time."

Catherine sat up, staring down at her husband.
"Jail? Lane, he's just a boy." She stood up and began
gathering bits and pieces of wrapping paper strewn
about the living room. "I don't want to talk about this
anymore."

"You have any plans for Taylor's third birthday?"
Lane watched the glow begin to brighten his wife's
face.

SIX

WIND OVER SMOOTH WATER

★ ★ ★

February grays the sky and dampens the soul of South Louisiana. Cold fronts, piling one on top of the other, rumble down from the northwest, bringing rain and cold air. Alternating with them, warm air masses slouch up from the Gulf, lingering longer, spilling heavier downpours on the swamps and lakes and the winter brown and sodden towns. In this unstable weather, track season begins.

★ ★ ★

"I love this weather!" Cassidy, dressed in LSU sweats, bent to his stretching exercises.

Caffey gazed upward at the swirling clouds. He shivered slightly as the February wind moaned across the ROTC drill field and down the long straightaway of the cinder track. "You got some strange ideas, Cass."

Cassidy grinned, his wheat-colored hair swirling about his head. "Just look at this!" He spread his arms toward the heavens. "All the clouds and cold and a storm blowing in . . . makes you feel alive, don't it?"

"Makes me cold."

Grabbing an ankle with both hands, Cassidy leaned his body along the length of his leg. "C'mon, let's take a warm-up lap or two, then you can come back and throw that shot put clean out of the stadium."

Caffey got to his feet, rubbing his hands together, and fell in beside Cassidy on the track. The two made an odd pair, strangely reminiscent of Brer Fox and Brer Bear as Caffey lumbered along next to Cassidy with his fluid and effortless stride.

"You know what, Cass?"

"No, I don't know what," Cassidy said, his arms swinging smoothly in time with his legs. He had learned long ago that arm motion was almost as important to a runner as his legs and with the help of Coach Mears had developed his natural talent into a nearly perfect combination of speed, power, and grace. "But I got a feeling I'm about to find out."

"I didn't think I'd be able to make it in college. You know, not smart enough."

Cassidy thought a few seconds, then decided to speak his mind. "You're a lot smarter than your daddy ever gave you credit for."

Caffey lumbered in silence, his neck bowed against the cold wind.

"I think he was the reason you never did much of anything in school. Always puttin' you down, calling you stupid all the time, telling you you'd never amount to a hill of beans."

"I miss him."

Cassidy thought of the big, greasy drunk passed out in the front porch swing, awaking in a drunken rage to bellow obscenities at his only child, and he wondered at the capacity of the human heart for love. "I know you do."

Caffey labored to stay alongside Cassidy. "It wudn't all his fault. Mama left him when I was just a little baby." He glanced up at the heavy clouds, the dark gray color of wet cement. "I don't think he ever stopped missing her."

"You're doin' real good out here, Caffey." Cassidy moved effortlessly over the cinders. "One *B*, two *C*'s, and two *D*'s. That's not bad at all. And you'll do even better this spring."

"Why's that?"

"One of the counselors assigned to the jocks is gonna help you out. Make sure you do okay with your grades."

"No kiddin'?"

"No kiddin'." Cassidy slipped easily into his role as Caffey's big brother, encouraging him as he had done since grade school. "They do it for all the athletes, especially the valuable ones like you who bring in a lot of points for the team."

"Why don't you just help me like last semester? I think I'd like that better."

"I'll be around," Cassidy assured him, "but they pay these guys to do this. Let him earn his money. Besides, we don't want to put him out of work."

Caffey's breathing had become slightly labored. "Nah. We don't wanna do that."

"I think I'm gonna stretch out a little, Caffey."

"Sure. I'm kinda tired anyway."

Cassidy glanced at the sweat suit stretched across his friend's huge bulk. "If I was carrying that much weight around, I couldn't make one lap."

"Come on over to the pit. Let's see how you do

chunkin' that piece of iron around."

"Not me. A man's gotta know what his limits are." Cassidy broke suddenly into a three-quarter-speed run, his legs stretching for distance, arms moving in perfect rhythm. His black spiked shoes appeared to barely touch the cinders as he glided along like wind over smooth water.

Caffey ambled over to the pit to practice his form in the shot put. He turned to watch his best friend run. Several of the other sprinters from LSU had fallen in with Cassidy, but he picked up his speed a notch and they fell behind. Even in practice Cassidy wouldn't allow himself to become part of the pack.

Coach Al Moreau, a tall, amiable, avuncular presence on the track, coached Caffey. They worked on form, speed on the turn, and timing—getting his legs, back, shoulders, and arm muscles working together in one all-out explosive effort that would send the sixteen-pound iron ball soaring toward that elusive sixty-foot mark.

"You're doing just fine, Sams." Moreau, his sweat shirt hood giving him the appearance of a cloistered monk with a fondness for college sports, patted Caffey on the back. "You're gonna win us some points this year." He turned and headed across the infield toward the opposite side of the track where the relay teams were practicing their hand-offs.

Caffey practiced another thirty minutes, then worked with the discus for an hour. After drinking several paper cups of water from an aluminum cooler, he sat down on the frost-burned winter grass to rest. Then he noticed Ginger Clesi seated in the bleachers, watching Cassidy as he practiced his starts, driving out of the blocks, his legs churning, arms pumping, body angling forward.

The wind coming off the Mississippi River a few hundred yards to the west of the track seemed to knife through Caffey's sweat shirt. He breathed in that unmistakable dampness in the air. Soon these leaden skies would open and send yet another soaking rain down on the city.

Practice was winding down for the day. Runners did their final stretching exercises, then gathered in groups of three or four, some walking singly, as they headed across the infield toward the locker room in North Stadium.

Caffey watched Cassidy walk over toward the low chain-link fence bordering the track. Ginger stepped down from the bleachers, her smile lighting a small portion of the gray day. After talking with her for a few seconds, Cassidy leaned over the fence and gave her a quick kiss on the cheek. Her face had clouded over, matching the skies above her.

Seeing the telltale sign, Caffey turned toward the gate on the opposite side of the track. *Yep. That's what I figured. And yep, there she is*. Seated beyond the fence on a concrete bench beneath the slick, bare tan limbs of a crepe myrtle, a yellow-haired girl wearing a black coat waited patiently. Beyond her a Bengal tiger named Mike prowled behind the iron bars of his cage.

Caffey watched Ginger, an almost visible pall of gloom hanging over her, walking in front of the bleachers, disappearing behind a tall hedge. Cassidy jogged toward him, his eyes settling on the blond girl in the distance.

As Cassidy sat down to take off his spikes, Caffey said, "Who's your new friend?"

Cassidy glanced in the direction of the tiger's cage. "Just a girl I met."

"You like her better than Ginger?"

"It's not a question of liking her better." Cassidy pulled his spikes off, slipping into his tennis shoes as he spoke. "She's just . . . somebody different, that's all."

"I like Ginger."

"You like everybody."

Caffey thought about that for a few seconds. "I think I probably like most people."

Cassidy stood up, his spiked running shoes dangling from his middle and forefingers. "C'mon, let's go get a shower and get out of here. I'll introduce you to DeDe." He waved at the blonde on the bench.

"D . . . D," Caffey repeated, watching the girl waving gaily. "Sounds like my math and history grades."

Cassidy gave a hearty laugh, taking his friend's big hand, helping him get up from the cold ground. "You made a joke, Caffey. A funny one, too. Maybe we could get you booked into some clubs. You know, a whole new career."

"I don't even have an old career."

"Look at this boy go!" Cassidy grinned and slapped him on the shoulder. "One one-liner after the other."

"It's not very nice."

A puzzled expression slipped across Cassidy's face. "What are you talkin' about now?"

"What you're doin' to Ginger."

"C'mon, Caffey." Cassidy waved to the blonde by the tiger's cage. "It's not like we're married or anything. There's nothing wrong with seeing two or three girls at one time."

"Or four or five or six," Caffey corrected him.

"That too."

"Why don't you just tell her you don't want to go steady?" Caffey watched the blonde stand up, fluffing her hair back with both hands. "Then you wouldn't have to lie to her and sneak around on her."

"You just don't understand women. If you give one all of your time, she starts taking you for granted." Cassidy glanced at the skies as the first heavy raindrops spattered on the sidewalk. "Then she dumps you."

"You the one's been doin' all the dumpin' . . . ever since I've known you."

"Gotta run. See you later in the dorm."

"You ain't gonna take a shower?"

Cassidy glanced back over his shoulder as he headed toward the blonde. "I'll clean up at DeDe's." He winked. "She's got her own apartment."

★ ★ ★

"Nine-five. The fastest time in the nation." Lane stared ahead at the two-lane blacktop, the white lines zipping past in the glare of his headlights.

Catherine gazed at her husband in the amber glow of the dash lights, his face beaming like a boy with a new puppy. "That's the second time you've told us that in the last ten minutes."

"It is?" Lane glanced over his shoulder at Cassidy and Caffey slouched in the backseat of the '57 Chevy. "How about fifty-eight-nine in the shot put, then? That's the second time I've said that, and I'm just as proud of Caffey. After all, he spent so much time at our house when he was growing up he's almost like a member of the family."

"There was times things got pretty rough at my house." Caffey nodded as he spoke. "I sure appreciate all those nights you let me stay with you."

"We were always glad to have you, Caffey," Catherine said. "You're a perfect gentleman."

Caffey's face colored slightly.

"I keep thinking about the '64 Olympics, Cath," Lane continued his track and field monologue. "How'd you like to take a trip to Tokyo? After all, we've got two Olympic prospects in the backseat of our car."

"Maybe just one, Mr. Temple. Al Oerter threw the discus one hundred eighty-four feet last summer to win the gold medal." Caffey's voice was a low rumble. "One-seventy is about the best I can do."

"You've got three more years, son," Lane encouraged him. "You'll just be hitting your peak when the '64 Summer Games roll around. Besides, the shot put's your best event."

Caffey said with his usual lack of confidence, "That's Dallas Long's specialty, too. Everybody's saying he's going to be the one to beat in the next Olympics."

"Not everybody, Caffey. I'm saying that *you're* going to be the one to beat." Lane grasped the steering wheel with both hands, stretching his back and shoulder muscles, then relaxed again with one hand holding the base of the wheel. "You're mighty quiet tonight, Cass."

"Nothing to say."

"Maybe you'd have rather gone back on the train with the rest of the team," Catherine said.

"Nah." Cassidy stared out the side window, his eyes remote. "I ain't much on all that rah, rah, team spirit stuff. This is just something I can do pretty well . . . so I do it."

"It's a team sport, Cass," Lane said. "You add up all the points each man makes at the end of the meet and whoever has the most wins . . . the team, not the individual."

"I win my own races. Nobody helps me do that."

Catherine gazed over the back of the seat at her

youngest child, thinking that he had always gone his own way, even as a boy. She suddenly realized why he had never played football or basketball . . . because the basis of the games was teamwork.

"Not in the relays," Lane said. "It takes four men to win a relay."

Cassidy glanced over at Caffey, who was staring at him with eyes that could see right through all his clever defenses. "Not for me."

"How do you figure that?"

"When I get that baton all I think about is beating the other anchor men to that tape. It's just me against them. Sometimes I'm in front . . . sometimes behind at the hand-off, but what counts is breaking that tape before any of them do."

"That's a strange way to look at it, Cass."

"Maybe so, but it keeps me from blaming anybody else if they don't run a good race and put me too far behind at the hand-off to win," Cassidy explained.

"I have to give you that much." Lane glanced at Catherine, who was still staring at Cassidy. "Coach Moreau told me you complain less than anybody he's ever coached."

"That's 'cause I run for myself. If it helps the team, fine. But if we lose a meet, the sun's still gonna come up in the morning and the world's still gonna keep turning."

"Why do you work so hard, then?"

"I hate gettin' beat . . . that's why. I just can't stand to see somebody else's back when I'm running. I'll do whatever it takes to see nothing but open daylight when I'm coming into that homestretch."

Catherine took great pleasure in the accomplishments of her children. And she suffered with them through their disappointments and hard times. Cassidy would always be the baby of the family in her eyes. With a mother's protective instinct, she had come to his defense countless times when he had been in the wrong, trying always to see the best in him, refusing to accept what her heart told her was there— something dark and violent.

As she stared at Cassidy, his eyes remote, staring out into the darkness, for the first time she recognized the thing at the heart of the fighting and the rebellion, the thing that had driven him all his life . . . pride. Pride that would not let him lose a race, pride that would not let him suffer any insult, pride that must be broken or it would one day destroy him.

Catherine knew the fearful consequences of pride from the scriptures: "Pride goeth before destruction . . ." But she also remembered the words of David. In the months to come they would become her prayer for Cassidy. "The sacrifices of God are a broken spirit: a broken and a contrite heart, O God, thou wilt not despise."

★ ★ ★

September. The very sound of it is cool. You can almost feel the crisp autumn winds and see leaves of gold and red and rust falling through the clear pale gold sunlight. But not in South Louisiana. September air still carries a July warmth with temperatures climbing into the nineties. Trees cling stubbornly to their leaves that abhor bright colors and finally sag and tumble downward in brown November.

September in Baton Rouge means football. In the white heat of afternoon practice fields, leather pops loudly in the sultry air as the offensive and defensive lines slam together. The quarterback steps into the pocket and flicks his arm. The ball spirals high against the hard blue sky on its way to the outstretched hands of a receiver. In the distance the band thunders the praises of its cleated and helmeted heroes.

Football is King of the Fall and the team quarterback its Crown Prince.

★ ★ ★

Alan Shepard was honored again today for having accomplished the first manned space flight for the United States back in May. His fifteen-minute flight in the Mercury module before returning to earth was highlighted with these profound words from President Kennedy: "I believe this nation should commit itself to achieving the goal, before this decade is out, of landing a man on the moon and returning him safely to earth."

"Kennedy's nuts! Send a man to the moon. He's living in a science-fiction novel."

Ginger sat on a quilt spread on the grassy slope of the levee listening to one of LSU's football players comment on the newscast. After practice a dozen or so had gathered there across from the campus for a beer party. Bare chested in cutoff jeans, they sprawled in the Friday afternoon sunshine among the scattered Falstaff and Regal cans, gold and glittering gladiators taking their ease before their first battle in Tiger Stadium on Saturday night.

Glancing back up the levee, Ginger opened her picnic hamper and began taking out sandwiches, pickles, fruit, and other items she had prepared for the outing she had talked Cassidy into. The gladiators continued their political discourse, spiced liberally with huge gulps of beer.

"Kennedy's the worst president this country's ever had. He's probably the one behind all them Freedom Riders coming down south."

"You got that right. All those riots over in Birmingham and Montgomery . . . stirrin' up trouble for no reason."

"We ain't got no worries over here. Jimmy Davis won't let that stuff happen in Louisiana."

"They oughta leave well enough alone . . . stay up in 'Yankeeland' eatin' their boiled meat and potatoes."

"Ain't that the truth. You ever try to get a decent meal anywhere up north? I think it must be a felony to put seasoning in food up there."

Leander Perez vows that Plaquemines Parish will never be desegregated. The fiery leader of Louisiana segregationists in a speech to—

"I'm tired of all this stupid talk. Let's get some music on this thing." A hulking defensive end with a black crew cut grabbed the radio and flicked the dial. From the radio's tinny-sounding speaker, Jimmy Clanton sang "Just a Dream."

"Now, there's a Baton Rouge boy who made it big. Number one song in the country a year or two ago."

"I think I'm seeing a dream right now." The quarterback, sitting cross-legged, took a long gulp of his beer and nodded toward Ginger. "And she's wearing white shorts."

"Yeah. She's a knockout, all right," the defensive end said with a nod. "I asked her out last year."

"How was she?"

"Wouldn't go."

"What?" Stunned and dismayed that any coed could turn down one of his teammates on the varsity squad, he asked, "Why wouldn't she?"

"Said she's going with Temple. You know, that bony kid that runs track."

The quarterback drained his can of Regal, then stood up. At six two, he weighed a hundred and ninety pounds. "Well, she doesn't know it yet, but this is her lucky day." He combed his thick brown hair back with the fingers of his left hand, grinned at his buddies, and sauntered over to the quilt.

Ginger saw him coming. Knowing his reputation as a ladies' man, she determined to get rid of him before Cassidy showed up and busied herself with the picnic.

"Hi, sweetheart. What's a nice girl like you doin' in a place like this?"

Ignoring him for a few seconds, Ginger saw that wasn't going to work. "I don't know what you mean," she said without looking up from her chores.

"You don't?" The quarterback sat on the edge of the quilt. "Why, there's a bunch of drunk football players right over there. Never can tell what a crazy bunch like that might do. You need somebody to look out for you."

Ginger kept her eyes averted from him. "No, thanks. My boyfriend's meeting me here."

"You mean that skinny little runt, Temple? You need a real man, sweetheart."

Topping the levee, Cassidy squinted into the afternoon sunlight and saw Ginger dutifully ignoring the quarterback. He could smell trouble in the air in much the same way he could detect the damp, coppery smell of a distant storm moving in. Putting on his best smile, he strolled down the levee toward the twosome on the blanket. "Hi, Ginger. We having company for supper?"

"No, he's just leaving." Ginger turned a strained smile in Cassidy's direction.

"And maybe he's not." The big, rangy quarterback made no move to get up.

Cassidy knew the privileged and protected status

of football players in the LSU hierarchy. His brother
had been one of them, and he had no desire to let this
one cost him his scholarship. "Stay then. We've got
plenty."

Ginger's jaw dropped slightly, then her face relaxed as she saw that Cassidy was keeping his promise
to her to avoid trouble. "Sure," she said with relief,
"let me get you a sandwich."

The quarterback was used to making quick decisions on the playing field as he looked for weaknesses
in the opposition. He made one then on the grassy
slope on the levee as he saw Cassidy back down from
his obvious challenge. "I don't think you understand,
Whitey."

Cassidy felt his good behavior sweeping away like
a piece of driftwood out in the swirling muddy currents of the Mississippi. With a benevolent smile he
slipped out of his leather-soled loafers and stood
barefoot on the quilt. "I guess not. Maybe you could
explain."

Standing up, the quarterback sized up his opponent, guessing that Cassidy was four inches shorter
and at least thirty pounds lighter. "There's only room
for two at this picnic." He glanced over his shoulder
at his buddies. "You're leaving."

Cassidy watched a half dozen of the football players, having seen their quarterback's signal, get up and
start walking toward them.

"Let's just leave, Cass." Ginger began frantically
gathering up the picnic items.

"No, sweetheart. The only one who's leaving is
Whitey."

Seeing there was no way out, Cassidy stepped in
front of the quarterback. "Leave while you still can."

The quarterback flinched visibly at the flat, deadly

sound of Cassidy's voice, then quickly recovered. "Are you nuts? There's six of us. We'll beat you to a pulp."

"Not before I splatter that perfect nose all over your pretty face." Cassidy's stance was relaxed, almost casual, as he spoke. "You really care what happens after that?"

The quarterback stared into the icy depths of Cassidy's eyes and somehow knew that was exactly what would happen to him. A cold blade of fear pricked his spine. He glanced at his teammates, waiting for him to make his move. "Nah! I'd be ashamed to fight a little runt like you."

Cassidy turned to Ginger. "I think we can leave now. We'll find another spot."

The quarterback looked at the smirks on the faces of his friends. Suddenly his pride overcame the fear. With Cassidy's eyes on Ginger, he swung a roundhouse right at Cassidy's jaw.

Years of street fighting had given Cassidy a sixth sense of danger. Combined with deer-quick reflexes, it gave him just enough edge to duck under the blow. The quarterback's big fist missed its intended mark, banging off Cassidy's skull just at the hairline.

Bright flashes of light exploded behind Cassidy's eyes as the blow glanced off his skull. But he was already turning his body toward his opponent, his legs uncoiling from a crouched position, his shoulders turning. He saw the fear in the quarterback's wide eyes just before the perfect nose became shorter and much wider.

After that Cassidy threw a few punches, heard a yelp or two of pain as they connected, then felt as though someone had overturned a truck full of logs onto him. Under the blows of hammerlike fists and kicks from heavily muscled legs, he felt himself plummeting downward into a smothering darkness.

SEVEN

THAT SAME ANGEL

★ ★ ★

Cassidy stood at the tall window, gazing with his one open eye at the students carrying armloads of books as they crisscrossed the campus on the way to classes. At his mother's insistence he had worn his dark blue suit to the LSU athletic department's disciplinary hearing.

"Why don't you sit down, Cass." Catherine sat on a brown leather sofa in the small antechamber, watching Lane pace the room. "They can't be much longer."

Lane took his jacket off, tossed it over the back of the couch, and loosened his tie. "I hope not. This is worse than waiting on a jury to come in."

Silent and sullen, Cassidy walked stiffly over to the couch. A grimace of pain testified to his three cracked ribs as he sat down next to his mother.

Catherine fought back tears as she gazed at her son. The left side of his face from eyebrow to jawbone was a mottled blotching of purple, yellow, and green, the eye still swollen completely shut. Crusty scabs darkened his lips and most of his chin. His right arm rested in a sling bearing the words "LSU Infirmary" in small black letters.

"I wish they'd get this thing over with." Lane continued to pace, glancing every few seconds at the double oak doors of the hearing room.

"Come sit with us." Catherine motioned to her husband. "It can't be much longer."

Just as Lane was about to sit down, the door opened, and Coach Moreau, looking ill at ease in a tweed jacket and brown tie, paused in the doorway, then walked slowly over to Cassidy.

Lane, a strained expression on his face, stood next to Catherine. With a reassuring pat, she placed her hand on Cassidy's arm. Cassidy stared blankly into the bad news already spoken by Moreau's slumped shoulders.

"What's the verdict, Coach?" Lane's attempt to sound optimistic failed miserably.

Moreau shook his head slowly back and forth, then stared at Cassidy. "They didn't kick you out of school. Probably because of the way you looked in the hearing room."

"That's good news, Cass." Catherine forced a smile and gave his arm a squeeze.

"But you can't run track for the spring season. They suspended you for a year."

"What?" Lane glanced back at the oak doors as though he would storm back into the hearing room. "Those thugs almost kill him and *he* gets a year's suspension!"

"The Alumni Association put a lot of pressure on them."

"And . . ."

Moreau rubbed the back of his neck with his left

hand. "And football is the biggest money-maker this school's got. The first-string quarterback got a broken hand out of this and—"

"He broke it on my son's head!"

"That didn't seem to matter much to them," Moreau continued. "What does matter is it's gonna hurt our chances for a bowl game . . . and probably cut down some on the attendance. All that costs the school money."

"All this is about money?"

"And prestige. There's a whole bunch of die-hard football fans that give the school a lot of money." Moreau stared out the window. "They take pride in a winning team, and when it doesn't win, they're not as loose with the dollars."

"Money. . ." Lane muttered. "What about a little fair play? What about justice?"

"You're a lawyer *and* a state representative," Moreau stated, giving Lane an oblique glance. "How much justice do you run into in court . . . or down at the Capitol?"

"Not nearly enough," Lane shot back. "What happened to the others?"

"Well, you already know that the quarterback's out till next year."

"And the rest?"

"Two weeks' suspension"—Moreau paused, glancing at the oak doors—"after the season's over."

"I'd like to give 'em a little justice!"

Catherine saw the muscles tightening along her husband's jawline. "Lane, for goodness' sake, settle down!"

Moreau stared down at Cassidy. "I worked it out so you can still train with the team, Cass. Don't let this thing get you down. You've still got your junior and senior years to run."

"That's right, Cass," Lane added. "You'll make the '64 Olympics yet."

Stifling a groan, Cassidy got up and walked across the room, disappearing down the hallway. His footsteps echoed with a hollow sound off the marble walls and high ceiling.

"He'll be all right, Coach." Lane's troubled expression didn't match the confident tone of his voice. "Thanks for standing up for him."

"Sure. We'll work things out." Moreau shook Lane's extended hand, then went back into the hearing room.

Catherine got up from the couch. "It's not fair, Lane. He didn't even start the fight."

"I know." Lane put his arm around his wife's shoulders as they followed after Cassidy. "I know."

★ ★ ★

Standing in his front yard, Caffey held a bucket in one hand and a brush in the other. He beamed at the gleaming new coat of paint that had changed his house from a shabby relic of gloom to a ray of sunshine.

"Just beautiful."

Caffey turned around, grinning at his best friend. "Ain't it, though?"

Cassidy gave it a critical eye. Hitching up the trousers to his suit, the coat and tie discarded at home, he strolled across the yard. "I might have used a lighter shade of yellow."

"Nah." Caffey's face glowed as he looked back at his handiwork. "This place needed something bright."

"It's that all right." Cassidy admired the changes

Caffey had made since his father's death. In addition to the much needed paint job, he had repaired the front porch, replaced the torn screens and broken windowpanes, and cut the weeds down so that there was now a respectable lawn beginning to come in. He had also removed the rusting hulk of an old Plymouth in the side yard and boarded up the garage his father had used as his mechanic shop. "You've done a good job here."

Caffey's face took on a benevolent frown as Cassidy came close enough for him to get a good look at the damage LSU's starting line had done. "Man, man! You look worse now than you did at the hospital."

"Thanks." Cassidy tried a grin but gave up on it. "I knew I could count on you to cheer me up."

"Sorry, Cass. I guess it hurts a lot, huh?"

"Only when I breathe."

"Huh?"

"Nothing. Just a takeoff on an old joke."

Caffey motioned toward the front door. "Want some iced tea? I made a big pitcher."

"I had something a little stronger in mind." He gently touched his swollen eye. "You know, for medicinal purposes."

"Don't have nothing stronger than tea."

"Not to worry." Cassidy turned and walked over to the black Chevy parked at the curb. Opening the door, he reached underneath the seat, lifting out a bottle stuck inside a brown paper bag, and headed for the house.

"It's real pretty, ain't it?" Caffey took one last look at his new paint job, then followed Cassidy inside.

At the kitchen table, Cassidy grabbed two glasses from the cabinet, hooked a chair out with his foot, and sat down. Pulling the cork out of the bottle, he poured the two jelly glasses half full of the dark amber liquid. "Take a load off, boy."

Caffey stared at his glass of bourbon with misgiving. "I don't know, Cass. Brother Dean says if you get drunk you can't go to heaven."

"You're starting to act like an old lady." Cassidy turned his glass up, swallowing and smacking his lips, although his eyes watered at the harsh bite of the bourbon. "You're gonna let that man take all the fun out of your life if you don't watch it."

Caffey sat down, holding the glass in both hands, turning it slowly around as though he couldn't quite decide whether to pour it down the drain or his throat. "I'd hate to miss heaven because of something that tastes as bad as this stuff."

"Let me assuage your fears, Caffey, old buddy." Cassidy took another swallow.

"Do what?"

" 'Assuage.' I learned that word in English 1-C. We college men talk like that."

Caffey seemed unimpressed with his friend's new word. "You're nineteen and you got one year in college."

"A minor detail." Cassidy took a third swallow, blowing his breath out. "The point is you apparently misunderstood the Right Reverend Dean's sermon. The Bible says that a *drunkard* can't go to heaven."

"It does?"

"Yep." Cassidy grinned, his blue eyes shining with alcohol. "And taking a few snorts of my bourbon hardly qualifies you as a certified drunkard."

"I reckon that's the truth." He lifted his glass, took a swallow, and made a face at Cassidy. "Boy, when you lay off awhile this stuff is really nasty."

"I joined the army."

Caffey stared at his friend as though he had spoken in ancient Hebrew. "You what?"

"Joined the army."

Taking another swallow of bourbon, Caffey shook his head and smacked his lips. "Ugh! You mean the ROTC?"

"We're both already in that. I mean the real United States Army."

"You mean like John Wayne storming the beaches at Iwo Jima . . . stuff like that?"

"Yep. Me and John Wayne."

"Why?"

Through the alcohol sheen, Cassidy's eyes glinted with a hard light. He took a big gulp from his glass. "They kicked me off the track team, Caffey."

Two shocks in less than a minute's time stunned Caffey's thought processes. "This is too much to handle, Cass. What about school?" He stared with unbelief at his friend who had been the only dependable thing in his life for almost a decade. Now he was shaken, afraid of what would happen to him with Cassidy off in the army somewhere . . . out of his life for good. "You told me you was gonna stick by me."

"Just settle down, partner." Cassidy propped his feet up on the table. "I'm not leaving till January. No reason I can't finish this semester."

"But I ain't got nobody else but you. You said you'd stick by me."

"I will, I will. I'll just be sticking by you in a barracks instead of a classroom."

"But . . ." Caffey frowned, still unable to handle the changes rushing pell-mell into his life. "But you'll be off at some army base, and I'll be—"

"You'll be right there with me."

"I'm going in, too?"

"Sure. I already talked to the recruiter about you." Cassidy took a pack of Camels out of his shirt pocket, tapped one out, and stuck it between his lips. Fumbling in his pockets for a match, he continued, "Told him about your grades and being on the track team and everything."

"Me . . . in the army?"

Cassidy got up, walked over to the cabinet, and found a box of kitchen matches. Taking several out, he flicked one into flame with his thumbnail and tossed the others on the table. "The sergeant said you'd be perfect."

"He really said that?"

Lighting his cigarette, Cassidy sucked the smoke deep into his lungs, then coughed loudly, his eyes watering. "This thing tastes like a piece of old rope."

Caffey found that he could still smile amid the confusion that had come into his life. "You just stuck 'em in your mouth without lightin' 'em for so long, I think you forgot how to smoke."

"Guess you're right," Cassidy agreed, looking at the cigarette as though it had just betrayed a confidence. "Don't have to worry about staying in shape now, though."

"You sure about this army thing, Cass?"

Cassidy tried a careful and smaller drag on his cigarette, managed not to cough, letting the smoke trail out of his nostrils. "I'm sure."

"But what about your scholarship?" Caffey shook his head and suddenly added, "What about *my* scholarship and the money I'm gettin' from Daddy's social security?"

Taking a hit on his glass of bourbon, Cassidy merely shrugged. "Uncle Sam's gonna take care of us. That sergeant down at the recruiting office said that the army would give us everything we need, and the money we make would just be for spending on anything extra we wanted. Sounds great, don't it?" He sucked smoke into his lungs, then blew three smoke rings, watching them drift upward, bending and twisting in the air currents. "Look, I can still do it."

Caffey shifted uneasily in his chair, drained his glass of bourbon, and stood up. He twisted the knob on the little white plastic radio over the sink, found a station, and sat back down. "This is all happening too fast for me."

"You're thinking too much. Just let things happen." Cassidy watched the trail of blue-white smoke rise from the tip of his cigarette. "You want to join up today?"

"Today?"

"Are you hard of hearing?"

"No."

"Well, quit repeating everything I ask you and just answer the question, then."

"No," Caffey blurted out. "I don't know. Maybe I oughta think about it for a while."

"Fine. You got plenty of time."

"I'll do it."

"Good." Cassidy hunched forward at the table, eyes narrowed. He threw furtive glances about the house, then he motioned Caffey closer with his forefinger. "Now I can give you the secret information. Kennedy's forming a special bunch in the army called the Green Berets."

"Who?"

"Kennedy. John Fitzgerald Kennedy. You know, Jackie's husband."

"Green Berets. That's some kind of a hat, ain't it?"

Cassidy took a final swallow of bourbon and

dropped his cigarette into the glass. It hissed out, sending a parting tendril of smoke curling above the table. "Listen to me now. We both got a year of college, and before we go in we'll have another semester. Plus we're both in good shape." He stood up and walked to the window, staring out at the abandoned mechanic shop. "The army likes athletes."

Caffey scraped his chair around on the linoleum floor. "I wish you'd get to the point."

Andy Williams was singing his heart out on the little radio on the windowsill. *We're after that same rainbow's end . . .*

The sudden realization of what he had done gave Cassidy a hollow, sick feeling, as though something was chewing away bits of his soul. Come January his books and track shoes would be replaced by an M–16 and combat boots. After the hearing he had dropped his mother off at the house, bought the bottle, and had a few drinks.

By chance he had driven past the recruiting office and seen the sergeant standing in the door looking like . . . John Wayne in his spit-and-polish uniform. Inside he had told Cassidy tales of heroism on the battlefield and of the bright future the army offered. "And the best part, Cass," the brotherly sergeant had put his arm around Cassidy's shoulder, "I can tell you from years of personal experience"—he lowered his voice to a conspiratorial whisper—"the women just love a man in uniform."

Now Cassidy's troubled mind fought for a way out, but he had closed and locked the door himself. Then he thought of what that group of toadies wearing coats and ties had done to him behind the double oak doors. *They can't treat me like that and get away with it. I'll show 'em. Without me and Caffey, they just lost their chance for the SEC championship.*

"You all right, Cass?"

"Huh?" Cassidy turned around, the old smile back on his face. "Sure." He went back to his chair. "Well, this is how the sergeant told it to me. Back in '52 the Army Special Forces was formed for counterinsurgency."

"What's that?"

Cassidy had hoped there would be no questions during his performance. "It's . . . it's when the army sends specially trained men into a country to help the people there fight anybody who's trying to do away with democracy and put in communism."

"We gotta fight communism for sure."

"Yeah." Cassidy shuddered. "You ever see them Russian women in the newsreels? They look like nightmares wearing feed sacks. We can't let that happen over here."

Pondering the effect of communism on the fashions and figures of LSU coeds, Caffey agreed with a slow nodding of his head. "We can't have that."

"Well, the sergeant said Kennedy's a real pal to the military, and he's forming up this crack unit called the Green Berets to go anywhere in the world where communism's trying to take over."

"Sounds like fun."

"Yeah. That's what I thought." Cassidy felt a twinge of guilt creeping into his consciousness. "You know, you don't have to join up just because I'm doing it."

"I know."

"You got your own house and the track scholarship . . . and the social security money and everything. You could go ahead and finish school."

Caffey looked around the room, then fastened his eyes on Cassidy. "You been my friend for a long time now, Cass." He stood up and walked through the kitchen door.

"Where you goin'?" Cassidy followed him through the living room and out onto the front porch.

Sitting down in the swing, Caffey stared out at his new grass, gradually taking over the bare spots of the lawn. "I 'member when Mama left. I wudn't but four or five. Then Daddy started drinkin'. Things got real bad after that."

Cassidy had heard the story many times but always let Caffey talk it out of his system when the urge came over him. "Tough times, huh?"

"After a while I got to feelin' there just wasn't no place for me in this world." Caffey's eyes mirrored the pain and loneliness of those years. "Then I met you that day."

"And we fought like two mad dogs."

Caffey laughed with a soft rumbling sound, his eyes growing brighter. "Yeah. Well, anyhow, you're the only real friend I ever had."

Cassidy stared at his bulky friend, possessing more strength than anyone he had ever seen, yet he had never seen him use it for violence except as a final resort. "We'll stick together, then, ol' buddy." A quick bright smile broke across his face. "And we'll have more good times than you ever thought about."

★ ★ ★

"You can't sleep, either?" Sharon, wearing a soft purple robe, walked into the living room carrying two steaming mugs of hot chocolate.

Cassidy sprawled on the gleaming hardwood floor, staring at the bubbling lights on the Christmas tree. He had on LSU warm-ups and thick white socks. "It's kinda nice after all the commotion's over with and everybody's gone home." The lights gleamed on his pale tousled hair. "I keep seeing other Christmases with these same lights and that same angel looking down on everything. We've had some good times in this family."

Cassidy seldom spoke of anything even remotely this sentimental, and Sharon felt fortunate to find him in such a mood. "Here. Try some of this." She handed him one of the mugs and sat down next to him, crossing her legs Indian fashion. "It's my secret recipe."

Grabbing a pillow, Cassidy placed it against the side of the couch and leaned back, crossing his legs and stretching them out in front of him. He took a sip of the chocolate. "Hey, that's good stuff? What's in it?"

"It wouldn't be a secret recipe if I told you, would it?" Sharon's soft brown eyes gleamed with mischief. "Besides, you've got so many girlfriends I'm sure at least one of them can fix hot chocolate this good."

Cassidy gazed at the lights, bubbling merrily with Christmas colors. "You're my favorite girl, sis."

"Sure."

"No, I mean it. I can talk to you when I can't talk to anybody else, not even Mama."

Sharon was surprised at her brother's casual comment. "What about Daddy? He's easy to talk to."

"Sure. He's a great guy." Cassidy took a swallow of chocolate. "It's just that . . . well, you know, I been in so much trouble over the years."

"Look what Dalton went through. You think that changed the way Daddy feels about him?"

Cassidy placed the mug on the floor next to him, crossing his arms over his chest. "No. But Dalton's always been Daddy's favorite. Everybody in the family knows that."

"Oh, you're just being silly."

"No, I'm not. It's the truth." Cassidy tried to smile, but it didn't work. "I don't mean that he hates me or anything, it's just that I'm not exactly his favorite person in the world. Especially after this last stunt I pulled."

Sharon turned a level gaze on her brother. "If you believe that, then you don't know much about our daddy . . . or much of anything else for that matter." Her voice revealed a trace of the iron core of her character. "Just because you don't understand how much he loves you . . . all of us, doesn't make it any less real. You need to think on this some, Cass."

"I guess you're right." He smiled wryly. "Jessie never was the perfect doting daughter, either. I think she tried to beat me out as the family black sheep there for a while. If it wasn't for marrying Austin, she'd probably still be chasing bright lights all over the world."

"She had her share of excitement all right."

"I think Mama really likes me, though."

Sharon stepped into the role she had chosen as Cassidy's part-time mother. "You know, if you're going to be a soldier you really should grow up some."

Cassidy's quick temper flared slightly. "Whatta you talking about?"

"I'll tell you *precisely* what I'm talking about." Sharon had never been intimidated by Cassidy's abrasive offensive tactics. "You sit around weighing Mama and Daddy's love on your own peculiar and unbalanced little scales like you were some kind of expert on the subject."

"Easy, sis, you'll blow a gasket."

But Sharon was on a roll. "Just how much love have you shown them? Love is more than a mushy,

gooey feeling you get once in a while. It's a commitment! You continue to love people and show love to
them whether you always *feel* like it or not."

"Whew!"

"And that's exactly what our mama and daddy
have always done for us."

Cassidy held his hands palms outward toward his
sister. "Okay, okay . . . you win!"

Sharon took a deep breath, let it out slowly, and
sipped her chocolate. "Good." Then she relaxed, letting her normally gentle nature take over once more.
"Little Cassidy, the soldier. What folly have you
wrought, good brother?"

"You know I don't understand them big words."

"That's another thing, Cass!" Sharon took off on
another tear. "Why do you act stupid all the time? You
think it makes you less of a man if people find out
you're smart?"

"Good grief! Here she goes again."

"I know you read novels and poetry all the time.
But you hide it like it was some kind of drug addic-
tion. There's nothing wrong with being literate."

"Fine. Send me a smoking jacket and a meer-
schaum pipe when I get to Fort Polk." Cassidy gave
her his best Laurence Olivier impression. "I'll gather
the boys around me right after bayonet practice and
read Shakespearean sonnets to them."

Sharon laughed her soft, musical laugh. "I never
could work up much anger toward you, Cass. And if I
managed it, you made me laugh it away."

"One of my many talents."

Sharon suddenly changed, a tiny crease of concern
appearing on her forehead. "You don't think you'll be
in any danger, do you, Cass?"

"From what? We aren't fighting any wars any-where that I know of."

"Well, I'm still going to ask God to keep an angel watching over you."

"I'm not sure that'll do."

"Why not?"

"Maybe you ought to ask for *two* angels."

EIGHT

DEEP AND DESPERATE

★ ★ ★

Catherine's breath formed a thin white cloud, blown quickly away in the gusting January wind. Rain splattered on the tin shed at the back of the Greyhound bus station. Out beyond the lines of buses and parked cars a horn wailed on a tugboat, invisible in the river mist, churning against the current toward the Esso docks up near the Earl K. Long bridge.

Staring at Cassidy and Caffey, wearing jeans and heavy jackets, she thought of them as boys, bursting in through her kitchen door after playing army in the backyard. Summer tanned and sweating, they downed tall glasses of strawberry Kool-Aid, jabbering excitedly about taking a beachhead or blowing up a pillbox, words learned listening to Lane and Coley reminiscing about their experiences in the South Pacific.

"You don't have to stay out here in the cold, Mama." Cassidy stood near several other young men, knapsacks slung across shoulders, cigarettes glowing

123

in the tin-colored light seeping through the clouds as they tried to look casual and nonchalant about facing the vast unknown of military life.

"Yes, ma'am," Caffey agreed, his grin as easy and natural as the flow of the river. "It's bad enough to have Mr. Temple down with the flu without you catching it, too." He slapped Cassidy on the back. "Hey, listen to me, I'm a poet."

"Housman's turning over in his grave right now."

"Who's that?"

Cassidy glanced out toward the river. "Just some guy I had to read for English class." He turned toward Catherine. "You're not cold, Mama?"

"Not much. It'll just be a few more minutes." She pointed toward the door of the terminal. "I believe this is your driver coming now."

Cassidy watched the driver in billed cap and raincoat trudge across the wet, glistening cement to the bus and climb the steps. In a few seconds he had the big diesel rumbling, dark gray smoke billowing out into the rain.

Catherine handed each boy a brown paper bag, neatly folded at the top. "Here's your lunches. Now, don't lose them. It's a long way to Fort Polk."

"No, ma'am. We won't." Caffey took the bag, unable to resist a peek inside.

"You boys be careful." Catherine found herself unable to think clearly, unable to transform the deep and desperate feelings of a mother's heart into words. She felt a sense of loss as though her youngest child was being ripped forever out of her life. Clearing her throat, she fought the tears pressing against the fragile surface of her self-control.

Cassidy grinned at his somber-faced mother. "Don't worry, Mama. I'm sure the drill sergeant's gonna tuck us in and read us a bedtime story every night."

Catherine forced a thin laugh. "If I know you, Cassidy Temple, you'll have him wishing he had never heard of the army in two weeks' time."

"Not me. I'm gonna be a model soldier." Cassidy clicked his heels together and snapped a salute. "Good conduct medals hanging all over my uniform."

"That'll be the day." Caffey pulled a sandwich wrapped in wax paper out of the brown bag and chewed it with obvious and noisy approval.

"Don't be shy, Caffey." Cassidy grinned at his mother. "Go ahead and have a bite to eat."

Catherine smiled in earnest as she watched her son's big, agreeable friend devour the first of four sandwiches she had fixed for his lunch. "Don't let him bother you, Caffey. If you're still hungry, just eat his, too." She remembered the countless times she had cooked for the two boys after school. At Caffey's house it was always hit or miss as to whether there would be anything on the table, but the Temple kitchen quickly became a haven where he could fill his stomach as well as his heart.

"Fort Polk Special." The driver stood in the door of his bus. "All you Audie Murphys climb aboard."

Catherine gave Caffey a big hug, then went up on tiptoe and kissed him on the cheek. "You take care of my little boy, Caffey. Keep him out of trouble."

His rough cheeks coloring slightly, Caffey grinned at Catherine, then looked down at the bag clutched in his big paw. "He looks out for me most of the time."

Turning toward her son, Catherine felt a tear spill over and slide down her cheek. She embraced Cassidy, holding him tightly, feeling the inexorable tug of the world pulling him out of her life. She wanted to speak, but the words stuck in her throat. Holding his face in her hands, she stared into his cornflower blue eyes, so like her own, then kissed him on the cheek.

Cassidy glanced around uneasily. "We gotta go now, Mama. I'll write real soon."

"Bye, Mrs. Temple." Caffey's broad face glowed with affection for the woman who had been the closest thing to a mother he had ever known. "Thanks for the lunch."

Catherine smiled and nodded. She watched the two young men walk across the wet pavement and disappear with other soon-to-be-soldiers into the waiting bus. Pulling the collar of her coat up, Catherine hurried over to her Chevy and climbed in.

Staring through the rain-streaked windshield, Catherine watched the Greyhound back out of its space, then straighten and rumble past her, its big tires sibilant on the rain-peppered, grease-stained drive. With a rumbling of its big engine, the bus climbed the ramp up to street level and turned right. Through the darkened glass of the bus window, Catherine recognized her son by the pale gleam of his hair, then he was gone.

★ ★ ★

"Fifteen hours to make a five-hour drive!" Cassidy rubbed his eyes lazily, standing up and stretching as he stepped into the aisle and followed the other scuffling, muttering passengers toward the bus door.

"I'm sleepy," Caffey offered, apparently feeling the need to explain his yawn.

"Yeah, I can't wait to get out to the base and get to bed." This said by a tall, gangly man who had gotten on the bus in Alexandria. His dark brown hair was a mass of curls. He stuck his bony hand toward Cassidy as he stood up. "Abe Jastram."

"Cassidy Temple. This is Caffey Sams." Cassidy glanced at the man's wild hair and wild dark eyes, trying to decide if he was eighteen or twenty-eight or somewhere in between. "Where you from?"

"New York City. Queens to be specific," he said in his flat nasal accent. "And you?"

"Baton Rouge."

"That means 'red stick.'" Caffey smiled, nodding slowly at his new friend.

"Interesting."

As they filed off the Greyhound at the makeshift terminal in Leesville, Cassidy saw a green bus parked at the curb beneath a streetlight. "I think our chauffeur's here."

A man in army uniform, his shoulder blazoned with three chevrons and forearm with hash marks, stood next to the door. His resemblance to Warren Barbay was uncanny, except for his age and the prematurely iron gray bristles on his head that passed for hair. The rumbling silence of his unspoken words split the midnight hush of the little town. Cassidy could feel the almost palpable gaze of the gunmetal eyes.

"I believe we're being summoned," Jastram said, apparently feeling the same thing Cassidy had. His small travel bag tucked beneath one arm, he strolled leisurely across the gravel toward the sergeant.

One by one the young men, averting their eyes, walked past the sergeant, climbed aboard the green bus, passed a pie-faced one-striper sitting behind the steering wheel, and found a seat. The sergeant sized up each of them with a professional grimace on his face, as though it caused him considerable pain to be in their undisciplined and un-uniformed presence.

When the men were seated, the sergeant, after a

scripted pause of thirty seconds, followed them aboard, closed the door, and stood as relaxed as a statue can get at the front of the bus. "I'm Sergeant Wilcutt. I'm army property. This bus is army property." He said it in a voice with a slight rasp but with the promise of abundant volume behind it. "And everything *in* this army green bus is army property."

"Not my nose." Jastram whispered the words out of the corner of his mouth.

Sitting across the aisle from him, Cassidy turned his head toward the sound. "What?"

"Everybody says I have my father's nose. So it can't belong to the army."

Suppressing a chuckle, Cassidy looked forward right into Wilcutt's belt buckle. He hadn't heard a sound in the two seconds his head had been turned.

"You wanna give this lecture, maggot?" The big man stared down directly at the nose in question.

Jastram turned his placid expression back on the sergeant. "Maggot? That's a bit extreme, isn't it?" He spoke as though practicing for the debate team. "I've been called 'Jew-boy' and 'beanpole,' but—"

"Give me twenty!" The sergeant's voice sounded like a blast from a tuba.

Jastram began fumbling for his wallet inside the pocket of his brown tweed jacket. "Okay, but I'm not sure I have twenty." He took it out and opened it, thumbing through the bills. "I remember a couple of fives and a few ones. . . ."

Speechless for the moment, Wilcutt's eyes bulged as he stared in disbelief. When he regained his voice, it thundered off the walls of the bus. "*Push-ups*, you idiot!"

"Oh . . . why didn't you say so?" Jastram stood up, took his jacket off, folded it carefully, and placed it over the back of the seat. He began loosening his tie.

"*Now!*" Wilcutt grabbed Jastram by the back of the neck, thrusting his body down in the aisle. As the sergeant stood above him, hands on his hips, Jastram struggled through the twenty push-ups and started to get up. The beefy hand clamped on to the boy's neck again, shoving him flat on his belly. "Anybody tell you to stand up?"

"I guess n—"

"Sir!" Wilcutt lifted Jastram's head at an awkward angle, screaming into his face. "The first word out of your maggot mouth is always 'sir.' " Then he pressed his face into the floor of the bus, holding it there.

"Sir," Jastram mumbled into the floor.

"Sir, what?" Wilcutt's booming voice had dropped to a hoarse whisper.

"Sir, no one told me to stand up."

"Excellent." Wilcutt straightened up, placing the sole of one gleaming combat boot on the back of Jastram's head. "Did the rest of you maggots learn something from this?"

Silence reigned in the dim and shadowy bus. A pickup rattled by outside the windows. Inside, heads turned, eyes wide, but not a word was spoken in reply to the question.

"Looks like all of your buddies went deaf." Wilcutt pressed down on Jastram's head, who uttered a muffled cry of pain. "Maybe if we wait here long enough somebody will have a vision, since they can't hear nothing."

"Sir, yes, sir." Cassidy's voice broke slightly as he answered the question.

"You must be prayin' down there, maggot." Wilcutt lifted his boot and turned on Cassidy. "Yes, sir, what?"

"I learned something."

Wilcutt gave Cassidy a cold stare, then looked around the bus. "Did anyone hear me say that 'I' was the first word *I* wanted to hear out of your maggot mouths?"

"Sir, no, sir." Immediately seven mouths chanted the words in unison.

"That's what I thought." He pointed to the floor, then turned his eyes on Cassidy. "Assume the position."

Cassidy remembered from ROTC that the "position" was the leaning rest position, hands and toes on the floor, back straight ready for push-ups. As he held himself off the floor with his arms extended, he stared straight at the back of Jastram's head, his eyes eighteen inches away. He wondered how the boy could keep his face pressed into the floor.

No order came for push-ups. Its engine roaring to life, the bus lurched forward with a grinding of gears, then settled down into a steady roar, its tires thrumming along the blacktop. Cassidy continued to stare at the wiry brown hair on the back of Jastram's head, his arms straining to keep the position. Soon his back and shoulders and arms burned with the effort to maintain the leaning rest position. No sound from Jastram, his face pressed against the floor, bouncing occasionally as the tires hit a pothole.

Ten minutes later, Cassidy's whole body ached and cried for relief. He felt as though hot wires had been inserted along his arms and down the length of his back. *I won't let him beat me. I'll stay like this all night.*

"Jastram. Temple. As you were."

Cassidy collapsed on the floor, then climbed back into his seat next to Caffey. *How did he know our names?* Looking over at Jastram in the dim light, he could see dark blotches on his nose and forehead.

As they rode through the darkness toward an improbable future, each of the young men was an island on his way to finding a common sea. The army would endeavor to make them all one big island whose very survival in the common and storm-tossed sea of basic training depended on functioning as a whole. All little islands would soon be taken by the sea.

Now they thought of a whole army of Wilcutts waiting for them at the base, planning an endless assortment of unspeakable tortures. In the rumbling bus they felt that the seminal creature with sergeant stripes was taking them off to a place of unending punishment for crimes they would never commit.

★ ★ ★

"Out! Out! Out!" Wilcutt bellowed the words as the bus squealed to a stop next to a huge warehouse looming in the semidarkness.

Eighteen pairs of shoes scuffled their way out of the bus and onto the macadam. The men milled about uneasily, taking in the vast, murky expanse of the base with its countless buildings and maze of streets.

"All right, girls," Wilcutt said conversationally, his hands clasped behind his back. "Let's see if you can form a straight line right here."

The nine young men, glancing at one another, shuffling their feet to get into position and readjusting their alignment several times, formed a modified S curve.

Wilcutt shook his head slowly back and forth as he approached them. "I thought I said a straight line, not an imitation of a snake with a crooked spine."

More shuffling around and muttering until the line resembled a flattened L.

"Splendid. Just splendid." Wilcutt paced back and

forth in front of the line. "You little girls managed to get off the bus without falling down. It looks to me like that's going to be the high point of your army careers." He stopped abruptly, stepping in front of a short, stocky, baby-faced boy wearing a mail-order suit and an expression of unbridled fear.

"What's your name, Stumpy?"

Cassidy felt certain that Wilcutt already knew all of their names. The question then had to do with some purpose other than information.

"My name's—"

Wilcutt clamped his hand over the boy's mouth, then smiled benignly. The fear slowly faded under the smile. "Idiot!" The booming voice instantly restored the fear. "Now"—Wilcutt's soothing voice now bothered the men more than the screaming—"what's the first word out of your mouth?"

"Zrrr . . ." the boy mumbled beneath the hard pressure of Wilcutt's hand.

"Zrrr . . ." Wilcutt repeated. "I'm not familiar with that particular expression. Would you repeat it?"

Taking a deep breath and shutting his eyes tightly, the boy tried again. "Sssshhh . . ."

Wilcutt took his hand away. "Don't know that one, either. Wanna try again?"

"S-sir, James Kennedy."

Wilcutt rubbed his chin between his thick, knotty thumb and forefinger. "You kin to the President?"

"Sir, no, sir."

"Well, don't think you're gonna get any special privileges just because you're kin to the President." He glanced at both sides of the ragged line. "You girls think Stumpy here should be treated different just 'cause he's kin to the President?"

"Sir, no, sir." They were beginning to get it right,

the hallowed words spoken almost in unison.

Wilcutt stepped back and continued his pacing, making a precise about-face when he reached each end of the line. The sound of a freight train wailed off in the distance like an anthem for the sense of loneliness and separation aching inside each man in the crooked line.

Finally stopping in front of Caffey, Wilcutt stepped forward and leaned until their faces were six inches apart. "Did your mama and daddy bother to give you a name when you were born?"

"Sir, yes, sir."

Cassidy let out an inward sigh of relief that Caffey had merely answered the sergeant's question without giving his name. He was beginning to catch on to the game.

Wilcutt realized it, too, then quickly spat out his next words. "Where you from?"

"Sir, Caffey Sams." Caffey had been too confident in anticipating the question. A pained expression flickered across his face as he realized it.

"Caffey Sams?" Wilcutt rubbed his chin again, shaking his head slowly back and forth. "Never heard of it. Is it close to Rhode Island?"

"Sir, no, sir."

"Where is it, then?"

"Sir..." Hemmed into a corner of his own making, Caffey's face went slack with the knowledge that the more he spoke the worse things would become.

"Don't know, huh?" Wilcutt's tone grew somber. "That's a shame when a sweet little girl like you don't know where she's from." He stepped backward and resumed his pacing. "Caffey Sams...." Stopping, he pointed at Caffey and said, "You sure it's not next to Rhode Island?"

"Sir, yes, sir."

"This is a real puzzler, this is." He ran his level gaze down the line. "Maybe your buddies can help you. I've found that the best thing for memory problems is push-ups. All you girls get down and give me twenty-five." He grinned at Caffey. "Except for you, of course."

A few groans and muttered curses in Caffey's direction ran down the line. As the men started kneeling down to assume the position, Wilcutt stopped them.

"As you were. Now the army way, which is the only way there is, for assuming the position is to throw your feet out behind you and land on your chest and toes and hands." Wilcutt demonstrated the movement, then snapped to attention. "The commands are 'get down' and 'get up.' Simple enough for most of you to understand. Let's try it."

Caffey stood at attention as the men around him prepared to batter themselves at Wilcutt's command.

"Get down."

They hit the pavement with cries of pain, skinned hands and knees, and torn clothes.

"Get up."

All struggled up, standing at attention. Most glowered at Caffey.

"Get down . . . get up." Wilcutt walked the line, making sure everyone was in the proper leaning rest position. "Get down, get up, get down."

As the men breathed heavily, holding themselves on toes and hands, Wilcutt stepped again in front of Caffey. "You remember where Caffey Sams is now?"

"No, sir."

"Okay, ladies, give me twenty-five."

★ ★ ★

Two hours later Cassidy collapsed on the top bunk of an open bay barracks he shared with thirty-nine other men. Three A.M. he listened to coughs, some muted conversations, and Caffey snoring loudly in the bunk beneath him. Wilcutt had shut himself in his room at the front of the barracks, light seeping beneath his door.

Cassidy thought of breakfast at home on Saturday morning with his family and the mounds of fried eggs and grits, bacon and sausage and homemade biscuits dripping with fresh butter and cups of steaming coffee . . . and the smiles and laughter and talk of the week past. *Love* . . . he seldom thought of the word except in an academic sense when he read poems or novels about it. Now he could see clearly what had been so important about those breakfasts . . . and so many other things he had taken for granted.

His mind turned to Friday nights at Hopper's after high school football games. Jerry Lee or Elvis would be blaring from the outdoor loudspeakers as the endless line of cars slowly cruised the U-shaped drive around the building and past the packed parking spots. He could taste the hamburgers and cherry Cokes and thick rich chocolate malts in tall heavy glasses and kisses in the backseat, lips cold and sweet.

A toilet flushed, sounding like a miniature Niagara Falls; someone padded down the aisle to his bunk. More coughing, beds creaking as men turned in their sleep or their search for sleep. Cassidy remembered how it felt breaking the tape with no one in sight on either side of him; felt again the warm sunshine as he lay on the grassy infield sweating, a pleasant ache running through his body. *No turning back now.*

PART THREE
★ ★ ★

THE TERROR BY NIGHT

NINE

WAR BABIES

★ ★ ★

The early days of spring had painted the LSU campus with brilliant color. Azaleas blossomed in vivid shades of crimson and pink and purple. New leaves on the live oaks glistened pale green in the afternoon sunlight. Sweet olive perfumed the air. The coeds also blossomed with the soft pastels of their spring wardrobes. Pale winter faces had been transformed by the rosy sun-touched glow of their skin.

Foster Hall stood amid the clamor of students changing classes, their conversations humming like nectar-mad bees lifting from the clover blossoms. With its red-tiled roof and graceful arches, the great stone hall retained the original Mediterranean look of the 1920s campus.

Cassidy sat on a concrete bench under the colonnade that ran the entire length of the building. He wore his just-issued army dress uniform and held an open *Morning Advocate* in his hands. Peering over the newspaper, he saw Ginger round the corner at the far end of the colonnade. With a hesitant smile she walked toward him beneath the lofty arches.

"You sure look nice in that pink dress," Cassidy said from behind his newspaper. "Pretty as a spring bouquet."

The comment caused Ginger's smile to flicker to life briefly. Then she forced it away.

"Says here that Kennedy admitted to two mistakes during his first year in office," he said as Ginger approached and sat down, placing her English Lit book between them on the bench.

"Really?" Although spring had burst forth around them, her words held a touch of winter.

"Yep," Cassidy continued, his smile slipping a little at the sound of her voice. "The first was Cuba, the second was letting the American people know that he reads a lot."

"Two whole months and you never answered even *one* of my letters."

Welcome home, Cassidy thought. Folding his newspaper, he laid it on the bench. "I wasn't at a Boy Scout camp, Ginger. The army didn't give us a whole lot of free time."

"Caffey wrote me."

He would. Cassidy leaned toward her. "How about a welcome-home kiss?"

"Three times." Ginger placed her fingertips beneath Cassidy's chin, stared into his eyes for two seconds, then kissed him quickly on the cheek.

"That's all I get?"

Ginger scooted back on the bench, taking in Cassidy's crew cut, the new uniform, his dress shoes, spit shined and gleaming like twin black mirrors. "I have to admit, I like the uniform."

"How about the guy inside it?"

Ginger's eyes softened slightly, but Cassidy was not to get off so easily. "Caffey told me y'all went into town on weekend passes. Time for that but not one letter."

"Ginger, I got enough lectures in basic training. Can't we just have a good time while I'm home?"

"Didn't you have enough good times in Leesville on your weekend passes?"

"No!" Cassidy blurted out, anger rising in his voice. "That place is packed full of GIs on leave. We had to stand in line thirty minutes just to get a watered-down malt." He remembered a dark, smoky bar with Hank Williams belting out "Hey, Good-Lookin' " on the jukebox, the smell of dime-store perfume, and stumbling around the bare cement dance floor with a woman wearing mascara as thick as paste. "Not a thing to do." His voice softened. "Except think about you every day."

Ginger gazed into Cassidy's eyes. His crew cut made him look like a high school freshman. Placing her book on the opposite side on the bench, she leaned over and kissed him softly on the lips, lingering as he touched her neck with his fingertips.

When she pulled away, the icy gleam in her eyes had vanished. A slight flush rose from her neck into her face. "I missed you, Cass . . . more than you know."

"And I missed you, too," Cassidy said, secure that he was back in her good graces. "Now, how about showing a soldier a good time before he goes off to war?"

"War? What war?"

Cassidy had heard Southeast Asia mentioned briefly during a class while he was in basic training but had quickly forgotten it. His words came from movie scripts rather than life. "Why do you think the army's giving us all this training?" He took her by the shoulders, staring directly into her eyes. "This . . . this could be our last time together, Ginger."

For just a second she believed him, and a slight shiver rippled along her spine, then she saw the smile tugging at the corners of his mouth. "You . . . you ought to be ashamed of yourself, Cassidy Temple." She placed her hands flat against his chest, shoving him away. "I almost believed you."

Cassidy burst into laughter. "Well, there might be a war . . . someday . . . somewhere."

Ginger pouted for five seconds, then slipped closer to him on the bench. "What did you do in the army, anyway?"

"Shined shoes, made bunks, mopped floors, scrubbed toilets . . . heroic things like that." Ginger's soft laughter felt like a soothing balm washing over Cassidy, cool and refreshing, after two months of DIs bellowing at him during most of his waking hours.

"I wish you hadn't left school, Cass." Sadness clouded Ginger's brown eyes.

"I'm coming back after I get out."

"That'll be three years."

"So . . . I'll only have five semesters left, and if I go during the summer I can graduate at twenty-four. And I'll still have eligibility to run track."

Ginger stood up, hugging her book against her chest with both hands as though shielding herself from an invisible enemy. "I'm talking about us! We'll be apart for three years!" A tear left a glistening trail down her cheek. "Do you ever think about anybody but yourself?"

Sliding off the bench, Cassidy gently pulled the book away, dropped it on the bench, and placed his hands at her waist. "I'm sorry."

"You should be!" Ginger brushed the corners of her eye with the back of her little finger. "I missed you so much, Cass. And now three years."

"I'll be home on leave, Ginger. It's not like I'm going off to a real war like my daddy did."

Ginger slid inside Cassidy's embrace, putting her arms around him. "I don't want to talk about it anymore."

Holding her close, Cassidy kissed her forehead, then her cheek, and finally, tilting her face upward with his fingertips beneath her chin, her lips.

A tiny man wearing a gray suit, horn-rimmed glasses, and carrying a brown leather briefcase walked past, his leather-soled shoes thudding dully on the concrete walkway. "Yes, sir. Spring has arrived."

Ginger pushed away, her face flushed.

The little man grinned at her, then at Cassidy as he continued on his way beneath the lofty arches. Out beyond Thomas Boyd Hall, the Memorial Tower began bonging out the hour.

"Goodness! I'll be late for class." Ginger grabbed her book, giving Cassidy a quick peck on the lips before hurrying away after the little man in the gray suit.

"Pick you up at the dorm at seven?"

Ginger stopped and turned around. Tilting her head to one side, she gave him a reflective look, then smiled her answer and turned away toward her class.

★ ★ ★

Crossing the campus, Cassidy caught the eyes of several coeds. "War Babies" raised during the Eisenhower years, they viewed soldiers as guardians of America's freedom and appeared more than a little enamored of this one's hard, lean form in a spanking new uniform. He stopped and held court with two who were friends and one who was a stranger but felt himself drawn toward the place that had been his joy . . . and his undoing.

Cassidy passed the Indian Mounds, walked down the hill to North Stadium, and found an open gate. Through a concrete corridor patterned with yellow sunlight, he saw two maintenance men in green work uniforms laying down white stripes on the field in preparation for the spring scrimmage.

Once inside the stadium, he made the long climb up steep tiers of steps to the top. Leaning on the concrete wall two hundred feet above Stadium Drive, he saw the sprawl of the campus far below—red-tiled roofs, green-lined walkways, and students ambling along as though they had an endless supply of youth and perfect spring days ahead of them.

Then he forced his gaze to the northwest, toward that gray-black oval of cinders that he had been unable to handle at ground level. Somehow it seemed more bearable and less a real part of his life from the dizzying height of the stadium. He gazed across the tops of the pine trees at the doll-like figures circling the track, sprinting down the straightaway, or hurling metal objects for distance. The muscles in his legs twitched instinctively at the occasional sharp crack of the starter's pistol.

Suddenly an image formed in Cassidy's mind. Sunday school class when he was ten years old: a table and straight-backed oak chairs, colorful pictures taped to the wall—David flinging his one smooth stone at a massive Goliath, Moses and the children of Israel standing on the shores of the Red Sea, and a boy about his age running down a path marked *Life* toward a distant finish line.

And the words of his teacher, Mr. Whitehead, came

to him about running the race, fighting the good fight, finishing the course. *Looks like you dropped out of this race, Cass, ol' boy*. He gazed again at the runners gliding like thoroughbreds around the track. *Maybe there's a way back for me . . . somehow. But where's the fight . . . and how do I finish the course if I can't even find it?*

Cassidy gazed westward beyond the infield and the bleachers toward the great yellow-brown sweep of the river, swollen with the spring thaw hundreds of miles north of this alluvial floodplain of swamps and bayous and coastal marshes. A sudden gust of March wind swept across the ROTC drill field to the north, sighed through the tops of the pines, and made a deep moaning sound inside the cavernous depths of the stadium.

Behind him, down below on the field, the two men stopped their work to gaze at the solitary soldier standing at the top of the stadium.

"Wonder what he's doing up there?"

"I think he's the one used to run track out here . . . till he got in that trouble."

"Yeah, I recognize his white hair now. Hated to see him go. That boy sho' could fly."

★ ★ ★

Wearing khakis and a light blue cotton shirt, Lane sat at his desk in the antique leather chair that Catherine had found at a shop on Royal Street in the French Quarter. Located at the rear of the house just off the kitchen, his narrow study held a wall-to-wall bookshelf crammed with the heavy tomes of the Louisiana civil and criminal statutes, biographies, novels, and a few books of poetry, including the collected works of William Butler Yeats and Dylan Thomas.

"Mama said you wanted to see me." Cassidy, mopping sweat from his face with a fluffy white towel, stuck his head around the corner of the doorframe.

Lane looked up from the legislation he was writing and leaned back in his chair. "Come on in, son."

Cassidy wore Converse tennis shoes, gym shorts, and a T-shirt plastered to his body with perspiration. Taking a swallow from a tall glass of iced tea, he sat down in a chair next to the desk. "What are you working on?"

"A bill to dedicate funding for higher education. The universities have been at the mercy of political whims too long. It's time they had some money in their budgets they can depend on from year to year."

"Probably won't pass," Cassidy muttered, taking a long drink of tea. He let his breath out in a rush. "Now, if you wanted to spend it on the football stadium or a new Rolls Royce for the coach, it'd probably fly right through."

"Not even twenty yet and you're already jaded." Lane picked up his legal pad, glanced at it, and tossed it back on the desk blotter. "Think I should go for the Rolls instead, huh?"

Cassidy draped the towel around his neck. His mind seemed to have already wandered off somewhere as he rubbed the cold glass against the side of his neck, then held it with both hands.

"Think you're in shape for airborne training?"

Staring into his glass, Cassidy shrugged. "I'll find out soon enough."

"Caffey told me you set a new record in the obstacle course up at Fort Polk."

"New course. Wasn't hard to do."

Lane found Cassidy's uncharacteristic modesty, tinged by a disinterest that bordered on apathy, surprising and somehow disturbing. *Maybe the army's dragging him out of his adolescent arrogance.*

Cassidy gazed at the framed black-and-white photographs hanging on the pecan-paneled wall on the opposite side of the desk. "You think I'm throwing my life away?" He then stared down into his glass as though searching for answers in the tinkling ice and dark, sweet tea.

"Serving your country is *never* throwing anything away," Lane answered without having to consider his reply. "It's giving something back."

Cassidy raised his eyes toward his father, the cloud lifting from his face. "You always know how to make me feel better, Daddy." He stared at a photograph of Lane standing next to the burned-out hulk of a landing craft. He wore his marine utilities, a three-day growth of stubble, and an expression of bone-grinding weariness. An M–1 carbine dangled casually from his left hand. Two of his buddies, carrying Garrands, flanked him. In the background coconut palms rose gracefully above the war-littered beaches of Guadalcanal. "I don't remember that picture being in here before."

Lane gazed at the photograph, creased and soiled in its black frame. His eyes then stared through and beyond it, back through the years. He could almost feel the breeze again off Sealark Channel behind the three young marines in the photograph, could almost hear their voices—then he stopped the memory as though switching off a movie projector. He looked back at his son. "I guess seeing you in your uniform brought back old memories."

Cassidy never remembered a time when his father had spoken of the horrors of war—only the friendships and the camaraderie and the courage. "These were your best buddies?"

"For a while," Lane said without explanation. "I had other friends after that"—he turned again toward the photograph—"but never as close as these."

"I had a good buddy in basic," Cassidy said, wanting to ask his father what had happened to his friends but respecting his reasons for not continuing the story. "Besides Caffey, that is. His name's Abe Jastram."

"What's he like?"

"Different from anybody I ever knew," Cassidy said, then drank from his water-beaded glass. "He's from Queens and he's real smart . . . I think his family's rich. His daddy's president of a bank. They moved out to Long Island a few years ago, but Abe still says he's from Queens." Cassidy smiled at a private thought. "The DIs thought he was a smart aleck for two or three weeks, then they found out that it's just his way. Most of them are from the south, so they're like us, but Abe just uses the language in a different way . . . kind of proper, I guess you'd say. Guess it's just the way he was brought up."

"He going to Fort Bragg with you?"

"Yep. Me and him and Caffey."

Lane picked up the legislation, holding it at arm's length, but his thoughts were elsewhere. "Airborne. That's a tough outfit. You and Caffey have been in sports a long time, so you oughta be in good shape, but this Abe fellow . . . he's pretty tough?"

"Tough enough to handle anything the DIs could throw at him. He's not real strong, but he can run all day and he's got great eyesight. Never picked up a gun in his life, and he shot the best score in our company. Even our DI finally admitted he'd make a pretty good soldier." Cassidy shook his head slowly. "You'd never know it to look at him, though. He's about six three and weighs maybe a hundred and sixty-five pounds." He looked at his father. "I don't think there's anything he's scared of, though."

"Pretty brave, huh?"

Cassidy rubbed his chin between thumb and fore-finger. "That's not it exactly. It's more like . . . I don't really know . . . more like he . . . just doesn't care one way or the other what happens to him. He's a lot of fun . . . makes you laugh all the time, but I kinda feel like inside he's not laughing at all."

"After he's around you and Caffey awhile, maybe y'all can help change that."

Shrugging, Cassidy finished his tea. "I think he's gonna be a good friend. Maybe that's enough without trying to change anything."

Lane looked at his son—young, strong, healthy, and full of promise. "You think this Green Beret busi-ness is really what you want, Cass?"

Cassidy nodded. "They say the communists are gonna take over South Vietnam if we don't do some-thing to help them. The ARVN needs us to help train them."

"ARVN?"

"The Army of the Republic of Vietnam."

"You ever hear of Dien Bien Phu, Cass?"

"No. What's that?"

"It's where the French finally met their . . . I guess you could call it their Waterloo in Vietnam. They gave up after that. Finally decided they couldn't win a war where they couldn't tell their friends from their ene-mies."

"That's the French for you, isn't it?" Cass said with the absolute certainty of youthful ignorance. "But we're Americans. That's the difference." He placed his glass on the desk blotter. "They let Hitler kick them all over the place. It took Americans to get their country back for them."

"This is a different situation, Cass. The Germans were in occupied countries. The Vietnamese are in their own country, and I'm not so sure they want anybody from the West trying to change the way they've lived for centuries."

"But the communists are going to make slaves of the whole country unless we do something about it!" Cassidy spoke in the jargon of the basic-training lectures. "Besides, we're only going to be concerned with counterinsurgency measures."

"That's it?"

"Sure. You act like you never heard of something like that before."

"I never heard much of anything about the kind of army you're talking about."

"What about Korea? You fought the communists over there, didn't you?"

Lane nodded. "A 'police action.' It always bothered me that they called it that. It was a war just like we fought in the South Pacific . . . only a lot colder." He stared at the slatted yellow light on the walls. "The North Korean and Chinese soldiers didn't care what the politicians called it. They tried to kill us just as hard as the Japanese did . . . and the men I lost are just as dead as the ones who died in World War II."

"This is completely different, Daddy." Cassidy tried to laugh it off, but it didn't quite ring true. "We'll just be acting as advisors mostly."

"Advisors, huh?"

"Yep. That's what they told us."

"Kennedy's reputation as a strong leader took a

pretty bad beating after that fiasco down at the Bay of Pigs. This Vietnam business may be his way of trying to put the shine back in his presidency."

Cassidy considered this for a few seconds. "Maybe that's part of it. Doesn't matter to me, though, as long as we're the good guys over there."

Lane nodded and gave Cassidy a thoughtful look. "One thing keeps coming back to me from Korea."

"What's that?"

"Something from one of MacArthur's many soliloquies. He said, 'There is no substitute for victory.' "

Cassidy gave his father a puzzled look. "Why would you fight a war if you didn't intend to win it?"

Lane saw no point in continuing the discussion of Far East geopolitics. He knew little about the subject and had never been one to second-guess his country's policies. "You think Caffey's going to get along all right?"

"Oh yeah! The DIs loved him in basic training," Cassidy said with fervor. "He's big and tough and does everything they tell him without any back talk. They all said he had what it takes to be a regular 'lifer.' "

"Look out for him, Cassidy." Lane's voice held a somber tone, his eyes fastened on Cassidy's.

"Sure, Daddy."

Lane opened the right-hand bottom drawer of his desk, took out an oblong object wrapped in soft, oil-stained cotton cloth, and laid it on the blotter. "Take this with you. It came in handy for me more than once."

Cassidy carefully unwrapped the cloth, taking out Lane's K-bar that had seen him through two wars. The heavy knife, its honed blade gleaming dully, felt somehow comforting as he gripped its ringed leather handle. "I thought I'd lost it out in the Basin somewhere years ago."

"You did," Lane said flatly. "I found it on the cleaning table about three years ago when I went fishing one Saturday by myself. Cleaned and oiled it and put it away for safekeeping. Hope you'll take better care of it now."

"Don't worry," Cassidy said with conviction. He remembered the time he had plunged the knife into the back of a black bear that was attacking Dalton. They had both come close to the edge that day. "The army taught me how important it is to take care of your weapons."

Lane's face brightened. "You've still got a few days left. How'd you like to go fishing?"

"Can Caffey come, too?"

For a moment Lane saw again the boy Cassidy had been, his blue eyes innocent and full of wonder. A sudden, sharp longing for those days caught like a barb inside his chest, then left him with a dull, empty aching. "Why not? He's part of the family." He stood up abruptly, rumpling Cassidy's damp hair as he walked past him into the kitchen. "C'mon, let's get some more of that tea."

TEN

DRIFTING IN THE
HEAVENS

★ ★ ★

A harsh whistle blasted Cassidy from sleep. He awakened to the sound of men rustling in their bunks, muttering curses in the ash-colored light seeping in through the windows, fumbling with belt buckles and buttons and boot strings. Still the blast of the DI's whistle insisted they were moving at a snail's pace.

Blurry scenes of the past night's taxi ride from the Fayetteville, North Carolina, airport to the base flickered in Cassidy's mind: garish billboards, pawnshops, tattoo parlors, trailer parks, used car lots, and bars with brightly colored tubes of neon twisting and turning against the darkness.

A voice bellowed between the whistle blasts. "You got two minutes to get out into the street. Uniform: T-shirts, gym shorts, and combat boots."

"It's kinda chilly to just be wearing a T-shirt and shorts," Caffey mumbled from the next bunk.

Abe Jastram yawned from the bunk above Cassidy. "I've got a feeling this guy is going to warm things up for us." He gazed sleepily down at the DI—tall, bronze skinned, massive chest, and shoulders—and added, "Rather quickly."

In less than a minute, most of the men had dressed and were fumbling through the darkness toward the light from the "head," spilling out into the hall at the far end of the barracks. Through the plate glass at the top of the double doors, Cassidy saw the DI, standing in the street in front of their barracks, a flashlight shining on his wristwatch.

As the last man fell into formation in front of the DI, the tall man glanced at his watch. "Six seconds slow. Everybody give me twenty!"

The men hit the blacktop immediately, did their twenty push-ups, and stood at attention. They had learned the lessons of basic training well.

"You always do one more and shout, 'One for Airborne!' " the DI said, his voice raspy and slow. "But then you 'legs' don't know much of anything, do you?"

"Sergeant . . ."

Cassidy stared at Abe Jastram, his hand raised high, and groaned inwardly. *Oh no! When will you ever learn to keep your mouth shut, Abe?*

Seeing Jastram's hand, the sergeant smiled benignly and pointed to him. "You have something to say, leg?"

"Sir, no one ever told us about the one extra push-up for Airborne." Jastram's face was as somber as the mood that had fallen over the men. "Therefore we had no way of knowing we were supposed to do it."

The big DI's voice suddenly took on a quiet, almost soothing tone. "Excellent point . . . by the way, what's your name?"

"Abe Jastram, sir."

"You'll have to excuse my lack of manners. I'm Sergeant Seabolt."

Some of the men rolled their eyes. All of them knew Seabolt was planning something extremely unpleasant for them, thanks to Jastram's big mouth.

"Well, Abe Jastram," the DI said as though he had been introduced to royalty, "why don't you come on up here and give the orders? We certainly can't have an intellectual like you doing push-ups with the peons."

Jastram instantly knew he had been duped. "That's all right, sir. I'll just do them right along with the other men."

"Oh, perish the thought. You might work up a drop or two of sweat. Maybe even strain a muscle. Couldn't have that now, could we?" He shook his head slowly as he surveyed the columns of soldiers. "No, sir, that's for these commoners. You're real special, Jastram."

Abe reluctantly left his place next to Cassidy and trudged up to the front of the platoon. He tried to look straight ahead but couldn't hold the cold stares of his buddies.

Seabolt grinned at Jastram, but the stony light in his eyes held firm. "Now, since none of these other legs had the good sense to question my order, I think you should double their push-ups. Forty—how's that sound?"

Abe felt afraid to open his mouth again for fear of bringing down more trouble on the platoon. He kept silent, head erect, throwing his eyes out of focus.

"Not enough, huh?" Seabolt said.

Fear clutched at Abe. "No, sir—I mean, yes, sir. Forty's enough, sir."

"No, you were right the first time, Jastram," Seabolt replied, looking thoughtfully at the columns of men.

"But I didn't say anything, sir."

Seabolt smiled and patted him on the back. "I know what you were thinking, though," he said, frowning at the platoon. "And you're absolutely right. This is a sorry-looking lot. Fifty push-ups might help whip them into shape." He turned to Abe. "You think fifty's enough?"

Abe knew there was no way out now. If he said no, then the number would increase and his buddies would despise him. If he said yes, they would merely dislike him intensely for adding ten additional push-ups to their quota. "Yes, sir."

Seabolt bellowed, "Hit it!"

All the men, including Abe, dropped to the black-top and began the push-ups.

"No, no, no!" Seabolt squatted next to Abe, his face only inches from his. "Not you, Jastram."

Abe got to his feet, standing at attention. In front of him the men grunted, breathing heavily as they did the required number of push-ups.

"No, sir, not you." Seabolt waved a big hand toward the platoon. "That's for the peons. You and I have much better things to do than all that grunting and sweating."

The men all finished within ten seconds of each other, shouting, "One for Airborne" and jumping to their feet. Except for Cassidy and Caffey, they all turned cold glares toward Abe, standing sheepishly next to his sergeant.

Then they ran to the chow hall. After that, they ran and ran and ran.

Cassidy felt that the whole base was built on a hill that had no downside . . . it seemed always up and up and up. He was soaked through. His combat boots, feeling as heavy as leaded diver's boots, squished with sweat that had poured down his legs. *Nobody runs this long without a rest!*

They ran. Cassidy's breath wheezed and rasped in his throat as he kept his eyes on the blurred image of the T-shirt in front of him. His lungs felt the size of marbles. He strained to force enough air into them. His chest burned as though someone was striking matches down inside him. No longer able to lift his arms, they flopped uselessly at his sides.

Nobody runs this long! Cassidy's legs were growing numb. They could have belonged to the man in front of him for all he knew.

The voice of Seabolt lashed across their backs like a leather whip. "Close up! Stay in step! Don't lag!"

When does he breathe? What I wouldn't give to punch his lights out!

Suddenly it was over. Cassidy stood with the others in ranks in front of the barracks, pouring sweat. Legs rubbery and wobbling, they managed to keep their feet. He glanced around. A third of the men were missing. Caffey and Abe were still with him . . . barely.

"Fall out! Breakfast in ten minutes."

The men that were left rubber-legged their way over to the barracks. Cassidy collapsed on his bunk, his breath still ragged in his chest. Five minutes later he was finally breathing normally again. Somebody said they had run eight miles.

★ ★ ★

"You girls gonna lay around all day?" Seabolt stood in the doorway. His sculpted body seemed to be soaking up the light filtering in the windows from outside.

Cassidy opened his eyes slowly, feeling as though he were coming out of a coma. The breakfast he had just downed felt like wet cement at the bottom of his stomach.

"Let's get this barracks in shape. You got exactly two hours." Seabolt gave the exhausted men a final appraisal, then pointed with a thick finger at Caffey. "Sams, you're barracks leader." Turning abruptly, he left.

"What does that mean?" Caffey raised up on one elbow, staring at Cassidy.

"Same thing it did in basic, Caffey," Cassidy explained, sliding his legs off the side of his mattress. He leaned his elbows on his knees. "You get to tell everybody what to do." Yawning deeply, he continued, "You also get chewed out by the DI every time something goes wrong."

Caffey's eyes revealed a sudden knowledge. He jumped up and stepped out into the aisle. "All right, everybody. Let's get busy and get this place in shape."

"Well, at least we get to be inside out of the sun," Abe observed as he struggled to sit up on the edge of his bunk. "That's one rational decision the army's made."

"You mean the army did something that makes sense?" a lean, dark-skinned man in the last bunk said to the ceiling and to nobody in particular.

"Sure," Abe continued. "They gave us PT while it was still dark and cool. In a couple of hours that sun's gonna make it tough to do anything physical out there."

In seconds men were pulling blankets tight over their mattresses, using military tucks at the corners to keep them snug. Then they began to police their areas, making sure everything was in its place in the footlockers and the hanging racks. Some men scrubbed the bathroom floor and polished the ceramic and stainless surfaces to a gloss. Others ran the heavy buffer, bringing the tiled floor to a high shine.

Two hours later, Caffey made his rounds of the barracks, checking to see that all was in proper military order as he had been taught in basic training.

Cassidy smiled at his longtime friend, proud of the changes he had seen in him over the past few months. Caffey had developed a confidence and self-assurance that Cassidy felt had been inside him all along and that the death of his father, along with army training, had brought to the surface.

Caffey nodded his head as he turned toward his own bunk. "Good work, men. Now maybe we'll get a rest."

Seabolt's shiny head popped through the door. "All right, Sams, get everybody ready for PT in five minutes."

When the heavy door slammed shut, groans rippled through the barracks.

"Is he kidding?"

"Either that or he's insane."

"No way I'm gonna do more PT now."

Caffey stood up and walked out into the center aisle. His bulky frame reflected in the polished floor. "You heard the man. Hit the street in five minutes." He stood there silent, arms folded across his massive chest until the men began struggling into gym shorts and combat boots.

Soaked through after the run to the parade ground, Cassidy lunged to the hard-packed dirt on command. All around him, his fellows-in-torture began the endless push-ups, then they switched to squat jumps and variations of physical torture that Seabolt must have stayed awake nights devising. After two hours, Seabolt formed them up in ranks.

Abe, sweat dripping off his long, hawkish nose, gave Cassidy a pitiful look. "Finally we get to hit the rack. I thought Seabolt would never stop," he whispered, but not quietly enough for the big sergeant's sharp ears.

"What's that back there, Jastram?" Seabolt turned his chilly smile in Abe's direction.

"Sir, nothing."

"Oh yes, Jastram. I heard what you said." Seabolt grinned at the platoon. "Your buddy Jastram said he's just full of energy and wants everybody to run some more."

Groans and muttered curses rumbled through the ranks of exhausted men.

"This is really gonna make me popular with the rest of the boys," Abe whispered as they began running toward the hot asphalt road. This time he spoke so that Seabolt couldn't hear him. "They're gonna kill me."

Cassidy gave him a cold stare. "If you don't learn to keep your mouth shut, I'll take care of it for them."

Seabolt's voice seemed an entity all its own—a grating sound born of pure air, a thing apart from the big sergeant's body, urging them on to greater and greater effort. It floated somewhere in the fog that had become Cassidy's world. His throat rasped as he tried to count cadence. The words would not squeeze past his swollen tongue. Unable to pull enough air down into his lungs to make sound, he gave up and tried only to breathe for one more lap . . . and then one more.

Suddenly the torture stopped. Cassidy's body trembled uncontrollably as he tried to stand erect on the hot blacktop in front of the barracks. His right leg twitched as though it had been connected to electrodes. Six laps. Six miles that seemed more like sixty ended.

His vision clearing slightly, Cassidy saw Abe down on his knees gasping for breath with Caffey next to him. Seabolt stood with hands on his hips, breathing easily, barely sweating. Only one third of the platoon was left.

"Eat a light lunch. All of you who finished will take a PT test at 1400 hours. If you pass the PT test, you'll start jump school next Monday."

Cassidy, Caffey, and Abe decided to eat no lunch at all, spending the entire two hours in their bunks flat on their backs. All three completed the exercise portion of the test. Ahead of them remained the final barrier to starting jump school . . . the four-mile run.

After three and a half miles, Cassidy saw two men ahead of him heading for the tape. Glancing behind him, he saw Abe loping doggedly along; farther back, Caffey was still holding his own.

Cassidy's legs were wobbling, but he turned on his last bit of energy. *I can't let them get to that tape ahead of me!* His lungs burned and his heart labored trying to pump oxygen to his starving muscles. Legs pumping as though underwater, he passed one man, seeing him as if in slow motion collapse to the pavement. *One more ahead of me. Turn it on!*

The tape beckoned. Suddenly, Cassidy could not feel his legs. Glancing down he saw that they still moved his body forward. One more man to catch. Now he was conscious only of a great roaring in his head. He saw the man ahead of him cross the finish line.

He beat me! He beat me! As he finished the course,

Cassidy saw a black mass rushing toward him. He held his arms up to fend it off. Pain stabbed his hands, his elbow, his hip. His vision slowly cleared to a strangely silent world as he watched Abe struggle toward the finish. Farther back, Caffey wobbled along after him, but the look on his face told Cassidy that his friend would finish in spite of the terrible toll on his body.

Gulping great gasps of air, Cassidy sat on the hot pavement, staring at the slender, fair-haired man, almost a twin of himself, who had beaten him.

★ ★ ★

Sunday afternoon was the only time the men held dear, the only lazy, indolent hours of their week. It was mostly spent lying around the barracks writing letters, napping, shining boots, playing poker, and engaging in that most military of pastimes, "bull sessions."

"Clandestine Communications . . ." said an ox of a man, Rufus Washburn from Pullman, Idaho, who was staring at the printed schedule of subjects Seabolt had given the men that morning after chapel. "I wonder what that means."

Abe sat on his bunk, back against the wall, reading the *New York Times*. He peered over his newspaper at Washburn's craggy face. "It means no loud talk, Washburn. We all have to whisper secrets in one another's ears."

"Map reading was kind of interesting," Caffey said, checking his board-stiff fatigues for loose threads, called "cables" by Seabolt and the other DIs. He hoped to head off the feud he could see brewing between Abe and Washburn.

Washburn turned his tiny dark eyes on Abe, who

had disappeared behind his newspaper. "You always got a smart answer for everything, Jastram. You don't know any more about it than I do." He turned his eyes again toward the sheet of paper in his heavy, callused hands. "Listen to this: Cryptography, Organizing Guerrilla Units, Methods of Interrogation, Psychological Warfare, Tactical Terrain Analysis, Fingerprinting . . . now we're supposed to be cops, I guess . . . Intelligence Nets—"

"You could use one of those, Washburn." Tired of Washburn's litany of subjects with accompanying commentary, Abe determined to shut him up. He had disliked the big cowboy from the mountains since Seabolt had paired them off in self-defense class and Abe had suffered several bruises and scrapes at his hands.

"Use what?"

"An intelligence net."

Washburn climbed down and walked over to the foot of Abe's bunk. "What's that supposed to mean?"

Abe crumpled the paper on his lap. "You could use it to catch yourself a bra—"

Cassidy stood up quickly and slapped his hand over Abe's mouth, then turned his eyes on Washburn. "He don't mean nothing, Washburn."

Abe jerked the hand away but listened to the silence of Cassidy's warning look.

Washburn turned his obsidian eyes back on Abe, nodding his head slowly. "All right, then. Just so long as he don't give me no more smart answers." He walked across the aisle, climbed up into his bunk, and continued to peruse the mysteries of special forces subject matter.

"You want that big ape to break you in two, Abe?" Cassidy lay back on his pillow, hands behind his head.

"I maybe could take him." Abe's voice did not hold the conviction of his words.

"Sure," Cassidy said, staring up at the bottom of Abe's mattress, "you might could flap your arms and fly to the moon, too."

"Yeah, maybe you're right."

"What'd you make of that lesson on torture and interrogation last week?"

Abe's voice sounded flat, as though he had purposely drained it of emotion. "Nobody can hold out. Everybody is going to break . . . eventually."

"Yeah." Cassidy pushed the methods of interrogation their instructor had discussed out of his thoughts. "We can't ever let ourselves be taken prisoner . . . ever."

"You think we'll go overseas?" Caffey sat across from Cassidy, rubbing the toes of his boots to a glossy shine with a ball of cotton he kept dipping into the lid of a shoe-polish can that was half filled with water. He had mostly ignored the scene between Abe and Washburn, hoping it would end without getting physical so he wouldn't have to step in as barracks chief.

Cassidy raised up on one elbow, watching Caffey work the polish in. "I don't think they're giving us these months of specialized training to keep us home."

Abe rustled his newspaper, turning briefly to check the stock market. "I talked to a guy yesterday at the NCO club who just got back from a *real* mission."

"How'd you get in?" Caffey asked, looking up from his work. "You're not an NCO."

"Well," Abe admitted reluctantly, "I actually talked to him out front when he was leaving. But he told me he'd been to Southeast Asia, all right."

Cassidy stood up, leaning against the iron bed

frame. "Well, what'd he say?"

Abe shook his head slowly. "Wouldn't tell me anything about it." He folded his newspaper carefully and tossed it to the foot of his bunk.

"That's all? He didn't tell you what it's like over there?"

"No." Abe sat up, dangling his long legs over the edge of his mattress. "He said we'd find out for ourselves."

As usual, Caffey chose to talk about the day-to-day goings-on rather than speculate on the future. "Y'all ready for that first jump? It oughta be great!"

★ ★ ★

The jumpmaster walked between the "sticks" of parachute-strapped men in the deafening roar and ovenlike heat of the C–119. "Is everybody going to jump?" he yelled through cupped hands.

"Yes, Sergeant!" they all roared back.

"What are you?"

"Airborne!"

"What?"

"Airborne!"

Cassidy let his eyes roam down the line of men across from him, the "stick" who would be jumping in the first pass over the drop zone. Each of them had white numbers painted on their helmets. Number twenty-one clenched the top of his reserve chute with whitened knuckles; twenty-three had his eyes closed, his lips moving in silent prayer; twenty-nine breathed with difficulty and seemed to be trying to stare through the floor of the 119 at the wispy clouds floating between him and the South Carolina soil far below.

The jumpmaster stepped to the door and looked

out, the skin on his face pushed back by the force of the wind. Then he showed his palm to the lines of men. "Get ready!"

Cassidy saw him mouth the words, the sound of them lost in the roar of the engines.

Now the palm turned upward, the outstretched arm raised. "Stand up!"

The lines of men stood up, hooking back the troop seats to the bulkhead.

The jumpmaster crooked his little finger, pumping his arm up and down. "Hook up!"

Cassidy glanced at Caffey, directly behind him—the second man who would jump in their "stick." Caffey hooked the snap of his static line onto the cable running overhead and slipped the small wire into the safety hole. Cassidy followed suit as did the rest of the men. Directly behind Caffey, he saw Abe's face, frozen in an expression halfway between joy and abject terror.

Cassidy's blood pounded in his ears, drowning out the sound of the engines.

The men ran through a final equipment check as the jumpmaster signaled, "Check static lines . . . check equipment . . ." He glanced through the door a final time, stared directly into Cassidy's eyes, then ordered, "Stand in the door!"

Cassidy stepped into the door, flinging the heavy snap on his static line to the end of the cable. He kept his eyes straight ahead, palms flat against the outside skin of the aircraft, one toe over the edge, knees bent. The blast of wind almost pushed him back into Caffey, who was standing directly behind him.

Waiting for the "go" signal, Cassidy gazed downward at a small community of frame houses with neat lawns. Cars moved slowly along a narrow road, peo-

ple walked down the sidewalks, someone rode a bi-
cycle. A large stand of dark green pine trees passed
beneath him. *Where's the DZ?*

Against the rules, Cassidy turned to look at the
jumpmaster. His lean brown face, crinkling in a smile,
was only inches from Cassidy's.

"How's it look, son?"

"Beautiful, sergeant!"

The smile widened. "Get ready, then."

Cassidy turned back to the bright, high world outside the baking warmth of the aircraft. The wind
drove the heat from his sweaty skin. The smooth skin
of the aircraft felt cool against the palm of his hand,
a rivet beneath the tip of his forefinger. Every nerve
tingled, burned with life. He wanted to sing to the
whole world.

Down below, a blue, winding river cut through the
green countryside, a blacktop highway, then sand and
tiny men moving around on the DZ.

"Go!"

Cassidy pushed off. "One thousand . . ." Suddenly
he found himself inside the howling roar of a dozen
hurricanes. "Two thousand . . ." The wind buffeted
him like a dry leaf, whipping him around. "Three
thousand . . ." A gentle tugging from above, the hur-
ricane vanished. Then silence . . . bright and pure and
endless quiet and a sense of peace.

Cassidy stared at the white puffy clouds floating
above and around him in the soft blue sky . . . his sky,
his clouds . . . drifting in the heavens. He glanced
down at the world, rising to meet him. *No! Let me stay
up here forever!*

ELEVEN

For I Am Undone

★ ★ ★

A hot wind blew in from the South China Sea. Dust swirled in yellow-brown clouds across the base. Office buildings, barracks, the EM club, even the chapel, were a sameness of white pine planking and corrugated metal. Only the makeshift stage, constructed the previous day, looked newer, its hammer-marred boards a shade brighter.

The mountains began on the other side of the sandbag bunkers and the razor wire and the flat, bulldozer-scraped land reaching the jungle. Covered in lush jade green growth, the mountains rose against a soft blue sky. In the distance, wreathed with mist, their color changed to a slate blue.

"This is great, ain't it?" Abe sat cross-legged on the hard-packed ground among hundreds of other fatigue-clad, excited, sweating young American men. "Our first month in-country and we get to see a USO show."

"Don't get your hopes up too much," Cassidy said,

glancing at the hastily built dressing rooms constructed along the rear edge of the stage. To the left
sat a five-piece band anchored by an upright piano
and a full set of drums. "My dad saw Bob Hope when
he was in Korea—said it was a great show." He
watched a green-painted helicopter clattering in over
the jungle toward the base. "But who wants to come
to a war nobody's ever heard of?"

Abe pointed his sharp nose directly at Cassidy's
face. "Let me have my little fantasies, will you? I got
a feeling we're gonna get a big dose of reality before
much longer."

"I'm ready to do anything to get off this base," Caffey said, stretching his legs out in front of him, his
boots gleaming in the slanting sunlight. "I didn't come
halfway around the world just to sit in more classes
listening to some E–2 tell me I gotta write letters to
my folks." He glanced at Cassidy, sitting next to him.
"I ain't got no folks to write to."

"Sure you do, Caffey. You got the same family I
do." Cassidy had come to accept over the years that
simply reassuring Caffey that he truly was a part of
their family could lift his spirits immeasurably.

Suddenly, the drummer gave a drum roll, followed
by a clashing of cymbals, and the band broke into a
lethargic version of Lloyd Price's big hit, "Personality." Five show girls wearing long, lacy dresses and
carrying parasols paraded out of the dressing room
on the right.

Abe's long face dipped another inch. "Is this the
best our country can offer its fighting men?"

After thirty seconds of minuet-like dancing by the
girls, the band cranked up the rhythm, the lethargy
disappearing along with the long dresses and parasols
and the girls' feigned coyness. Clad now in abbrevi-

ated chemises dripping with ribbons and bows, they sashayed across the stage, pointing out individual men in the audience, singing as though each of them was the only man left in the world: "'Cause you've got personality . . ."

None of the five sang to Cassidy, but he heard his own special melody anyway as he fastened his eyes on the girl in the middle. *Her hair's the same color as my mother's* was his fifth or sixth thought. He took in the smooth ivory shading of her skin, her finely molded features, the intricate slopes and turnings of her face and form, then found himself captivated by her expressive deep blue eyes.

Another song, some more dancing, then a comedian pranced onstage and bantered with the girls and his audience of entertainment-starved GIs. Cassidy's mind took in little of the performance. He wondered what it would be like to have this beautiful and bouncy blonde all to himself. He imagined himself back home, breaking the tape at the SEC finals, winning the hundred-yard dash, then turning to see her in the bleachers cheering for him. . . . Then he realized that every man in the outfit would try to hit on her when the show was over.

"Hey, where you going?" Caffey watched Cassidy stand up and begin threading his way carefully through the seated men, still enthralled with the performance.

Glancing back, he said, "Got something to do. See you after the show."

★ ★ ★

Cassidy stood at the foot of the stairs behind the stage. He wore his only set of freshly starched fatigues, a webbed gun belt minus the holster and .45

automatic, and the black-and-white armbands of the Military Police. When the band played the final fanfare, he watched the girls hurry around the wooden barrier and into their makeshift dressing room. In a few minutes they emerged, talking excitedly, wearing spanking new standard-issue fatigues and white tennis shoes.

As they began filing down the stairs, Cassidy said, "Excuse me, miss . . ."

The blond girl turned surprised eyes on the lean, bronzed soldier with the startlingly sun-bleached hair and clear blue eyes. "Yes . . ."

"My name's Cassidy Temple and I've been assigned as your escort." Cassidy turned on his best tomcat smile. "You know . . . for your protection."

The girl watched her friends pass by, following the troupe manager, a middle-aged man wearing a seersucker suit and a snap-brimmed hat. Then she gave Cassidy a dubious look. "Well, Mr. Temple, why do I get the impression that the only protection I need . . . is protection from you?"

Cassidy's grin widened, but he found that words somehow escaped him and he only shrugged in reply.

The girl glanced toward the departing troupe and beyond at the eager hangers-on waiting to meet them. "And why doesn't anyone else have an escort?" she added, giving him the once-over. "For their own protection, of course."

Cassidy gave her a hangdog look. " 'Woe is me! for I am undone . . .' "

"Undone?" she repeated, a crease forming between her finely formed eyebrows. "Why, that sounds positively biblical. Are you some kind of preacher?"

Laughing out loud, Cassidy shook his head. "I don't think you'd find anybody to back you up on that." He watched the manager and his flock disappear around the corner of a building. "Just part of a verse I remembered from Sunday school. It's from Isaiah. Something I learned for a part in a play." Thinking of that faraway room hung with colorful pictures of Moses and David and Jesus, bidding the little children to come to Him, he said, "That seems like a hundred years ago."

"I'm Linda Spring." She held out her hand, the nails shaped to perfection and glossy with clear polish.

Cassidy took her hand. A warmth seemed to radiate from it, leaving a tingling feeling on his palm. "Why'd you decide to tell me your name?"

"Your accent, for one thing." Linda took his arm as they followed the path of her friends.

"No kidding?"

"Sure. A southern boy who goes to Sunday school and memorizes Bible verses can't be all *that* bad." Her smile was warm and genuine. "Besides, I like those little cloth wings on your left pocket. Does that mean you can fly?"

Cassidy thought of the weeks of harassment and physical misery that had earned him the right to wear the Airborne insignia and said, "Not quite . . . but close to it."

"Well, maybe you could fly me over to the mess hall, Mr. Cassidy Temple. Word has it they're going to feed us, and I'm simply famished."

"Why don't we drop this *Mr.* business?" Cassidy said, noticing that her deep blue eyes on closer inspection held tiny flecks of violet color.

"Okay, Preacher, and you can call me Linda."

Cassidy flinched slightly at the nickname she had chosen for him. "Good. Linda, you don't want to eat in that mess hall, believe me."

"And what did you have in mind for us?" The corners of her eyes crinkled slightly with her smile. "Considering the way you quote Isaiah, I hope it's not a fast."

Cassidy slipped his armbands off and put them in a cargo pocket of his fatigues, then unhooked the gun belt and fastened it underneath his shirt. Taking Linda's arm, he said, "No sense in pushing my luck with this costume," as they walked toward the base's main road constructed of mats of perforated metal laid end-to-end. Walking through the main gate, Cassidy threw a casual wave to the guard. "He and I were at Fort Polk together."

"So he lets you just walk on through?"

"Why not? Nothing's happening around here anyway."

Linda eased his hand away from her arm. "You never told me what you had in mind to replace the mess hall."

Cassidy felt surprised and a little disheartened when Linda took his hand from her arm. He tried but couldn't remember a time when that had happened before. "I'm a Sunday school boy, remember? You can trust me."

"Well, I may try you just this one time," Linda said, slipping her hand inside his arm.

Peasant shacks made of scrap lumber and rusted sheets of tin lined the green fields alongside the road. Women wearing conical straw hats squatted in front of their huts or out in the rice paddies. Water buffalo rolled in mudholes. Half-naked children played alongside the road, yelling at the passersby on bicycles, Honda motorbikes, and an assortment of military vehicles.

A heavy canvas-covered truck rumbled past them on the dirt road. GIs waved out the back, openly expressing their admiration for Linda.

She waved back, her smile encouraging them to cheers and hoots of joy. "Looks like the morale of the men over here is pretty good."

Cassidy watched the truck bump along the rutted road, then abruptly turn into the base. He experienced a sudden protective attitude toward Linda that he had never felt before with any other woman. It concerned him, but he brushed it off, attributing it to the several thousand men in and around the base who would like to be in his place.

"Are you still with me?" Linda asked. "Do you think it's good?"

"What?"

"The morale."

Cassidy glanced at a jeep bumping along past them. Two officers sitting in the backseat openly admired the girl on his arm. "Well, I can't speak for the other men, but mine's sure improved in the last ten minutes."

Smiling, Linda gave his arm a slight squeeze. "How long have you been over here?"

"Twenty-seven days."

"What do you think?"

"Big question," Cassidy said, thinking of the dull, dry days sitting in classrooms or sweating out the physical training that had become a normal part of his existence. "We're learning to work with our Vietnamese counterparts. Their scouts are pretty good, but from what I've heard so far, the ARVN couldn't stand up to a troop of Boy Scouts."

"ARVN?"

"The Army of the Republic of Vietnam."

Linda had apparently reached her capacity for new military information. "You still haven't told me where we're going to eat, Preacher."

"Funny you should ask." Cassidy pointed to an openside shanty on the side of the road. Constructed of scrap lumber and a thatched roof of split palm fronds, it called to mind the house made of sticks from the story of the "Three Little Pigs."

"We're eating there?" Linda glanced back toward the base. "I think the mess hall would be safer."

"Trust me."

Linda gazed at the tall, slender palm trees and the slate blue sea capping in the wind beyond the coast road. "Well, at least the scenery's nice."

They sat down on split-cane stools at the little food stand. Behind the counter a tiny woman dressed in loose white pants and a flowered cotton blouse squatted in front of a small propane stove. All four burners held skillets and pots. Turning around toward her guests, she smiled at them with her five teeth stained as black as her clothes.

"She's kinda cute, ain't she?" Cassidy said to Linda. He smiled back, nodded, and held up two fingers.

Without a word the woman turned to her stove and began filling two battered army mess hall trays with steaming food from her pots. Then opening a huge ice chest resting on wooden blocks, she served salad into one of the sections of the trays.

"What's her name?"

Cassidy shrugged. "I've never heard her say a word. Doesn't hurt her business, though."

"How's that?"

"She only cooks one dish each day," Cassidy explained. "You take it or leave it." He rubbed his chin.

"Sometimes, though, I think she understands everything we're saying."

The woman set their plates on the counter, then squatted at her stove, stirring the contents of the pots, occasionally adjusting the burners on the stove.

Linda inspected the knife and fork. "How'd she get the trays and flatware? They're from the base. And look at that." She pointed to several brass shell casings standing on a shelf on the back wall. They held bright flowers.

Cassidy stabbed his fork into a tender piece of chicken, thickly coated with curry sauce. "Beats me. I've seen about as much government issue outside the base as inside. The black market over here is kind of like the weather."

"The weather?"

"Yeah. Everybody talks about it, but nobody ever does anything about it." He took a bite. "Umm . . . you gotta try this curried chicken."

Linda poked around in her salad—crisp lettuce, bright red tomatoes, and hard-boiled eggs sliced as thin as wafers. Then she took a careful bite of chicken. A curry-sauce smile broke out on her face. "This is great! I guess I made the right choice to trust you, after all."

Cassidy watched her eat in silence, enjoying the obvious pleasure she took in the food. The little woman in black, noticing the lack of conversation, turned around. He gave her the thumbs-up sign, and she smiled. Pulling out a little stool with a woven seat, she sat on it and thumbed through a year-old *Life* magazine.

★ ★ ★

Linda gazed at the sun, a bright red smudge rest-

177

ing on the distant mountains. Above her the palms swayed gracefully in the sea breeze. A frothy surf slipped across her bare feet as she walked next to Cassidy along the beach. "This is so lovely!" She slipped her hand in his. "I'm glad you went to all that trouble to act like my escort."

"Shucks, ma'am." Cassidy gave his redneck chuckle and kicked at the water. "Just doing my duty for good ol' Uncle Sam." He smiled, watching her hair like fine corn silk swirling about her face. "Where're you from, Linda?"

"Chicago."

"I thought I picked up a Yankee accent."

Linda blew her breath out in a sigh. Shaking her head, she said, "And I thought all those diction lessons had finally gotten me over that."

"Why would you want to get over it?"

"I'd like to get into films, and it's easier if you can talk like the man on the six o'clock news." The sea breeze whisked away the soft sigh that escaped her lips. "I should have known better. My dad's been with the state department twenty years, traveled all over the world, and he still has the accent."

"Films?"

"You know, movies."

Cassidy watched a navy gunboat bouncing along in the whitecaps, hugging the coastline as it headed south. "You sound like my sister."

"Really?"

"Yeah. She went to Hollywood, then to Korea on a USO trip with Bob Hope."

Linda stopped, gazing at Cassidy with a strange gleam, almost a glitter in her eyes. "No kidding? Bob Hope? That's great! Did she make any movies?"

"Nah. She gave it all up."

"What for?" Linda seemed stunned by the news about someone she didn't even know.

"She said there were too many . . . *compromises*, I believe is the word she used. Now she has a husband and a little boy. He's four years old."

Linda nodded her head sagely. "I don't blame her for that, but I don't think I could ever just *give up*. Not as long as there was still a chance to make it somewhere in show business."

Cassidy felt a sudden disappointment at Linda's words. *Why should I care if she doesn't give up show business?* "Oh, she kept at it awhile longer before she decided to trade it in for the ol' ball and chain," he continued. "Went to Memphis back when Elvis was first getting popular. Wanted to be a rock-and-roll singer. That didn't work out, either."

"How's she getting along?" Linda sounded as though she were inquiring about the health of a very ill patient. "I mean . . . is she happy?"

Cassidy gazed at Linda's almost distraught expression and laughed. "Are you kidding? She wouldn't trade places with Jackie Kennedy."

"Oh." Linda brushed aside the news of Jessie's failure in show business. "Now, how about you, Preacher? You have any deep dark secrets I should know about?"

"Only one."

"And what would that be?"

Cassidy stepped close to her, put his arm around her waist, and kissed her on the lips before she could protest. Linda placed the flat of her hands against his chest to push him away, then let them relax and returned his kiss with a sudden and unexpected passion. When the kiss ended, she gazed up at him, brushing stray tendrils of hair back from her flushed face. "Well . . . I've never had a question answered quite like that before."

★ ★ ★

"She's all right." Hands clasped behind his head, Cassidy lay on his bunk in the four-man room he and Caffey shared with Abe and Washburn.

Caffey used a soft cotton cloth attached to the end of a slim rod to clean the barrel of his M–16. "Whaddya mean, 'all right'? You never talked about a girl this much in your life." A small record player holding a stack of 45s sat on a table next to his bed. It played the Shirelles latest hit, "Soldier Boy."

"She's fun."

" 'Fun.' A puppy is fun; fishin' is fun." Caffey squirted oil on the rag and ran it back through the barrel. "You've seen her every night for the past two weeks."

Cassidy had never admitted to any real affection for his girlfriends and refused to change his ways at the age of twenty. "Not much variety around here."

"Oh yeah. Well, you went through about a dozen of those army nurses before Linda showed up." Caffey enjoyed making his friend squirm after all the years he had seen him mesmerize one girlfriend after the other and usually two or three at a time. "I think this one's got your number, Cass."

"You're crazy!" Cassidy pushed himself off the bunk. "Besides, she's got this thing about making it in show business. No time for marriage."

"Marriage?"

Cassidy's face paled slightly, then grew warm. He turned away, staring out the window.

"Did I hear you say the forbidden word?"

"What word?"

Still holding on to the rifle barrel, Caffey rolled back on his mattress and broke into a rumbling laughter. "This *is* the real thing. I never thought I'd see the day Cassidy Temple would actually fall in love."

Cassidy turned around, watching his big friend shaking with laughter, tears filling his eyes. "You're really having a good time with this, aren't you, Caffey?"

Sitting up and wiping his eyes with the back of his hand, he said, "Why? What makes you say that?" Then the laughter started again.

After Caffey had gained control of himself, Cassidy sat down in a metal folding chair next to a writing desk attached to the wall. "Okay. We did talk about marriage for the first time last night." He took a deep breath. "But it wasn't anything really, you know, serious."

"Nah! Marriage isn't serious? It's just spending the rest of your life with somebody." Laughter welled up in Caffey's belly, shoving the corners of his mouth upward, crinkling his eyes.

"Don't you start again!"

Caffey swallowed the laugh. "How much longer is she going to be here?"

"Four or five more weeks maybe. When they finish touring the bases down here, they're going to do a few shows for the navy out on some of the ships." Then he hastened to add, "But they'll always come back here to spend the night."

"Uh-huh."

"She's really something, Caffey."

"Uh-huh."

"Is that all you can say?"

"I think we're gonna get our first mission before too long." Caffey began reassembling his weapon.

181

"How do you know?" Cassidy leaned forward in his chair, staring directly into his friend's eyes.

Caffey grinned back. "'Cause I don't go courtin' every night. Hang around in the right places with the right people and you pick up things."

Cassidy ignored the remark.

"What do you think about this Strategic Hamlet Program the government's starting?"

Cassidy watched the little 45 record-changer drop another record onto the turntable. The Kingston Trio sang "Where Have All the Flowers Gone?" "I think a little moat around the villages and a few pungie sticks ain't gonna stop the Vietcong."

Nodding his agreement, Caffey continued fitting the pieces of his rifle together with a practiced hand.

"What else did you hear?"

"Sergeant Tree, you know the guy who taught us some classes, just may be on our team."

"Yeah, he knew what he was talkin' about. Stuff that could keep us alive." Cassidy grew more excited at the prospect of actually flying out to the jungle on a mission. "Not like that 'Winning Hearts and Minds' baloney. As far as I'm concerned, those classes were worthless."

"They didn't even make sense to me. If the people out in those villages don't think we have any business over here, all the talk in the world ain't gonna help."

Cassidy's eyes narrowed. Glancing out the window at a passing Lambretta covered with a heavy green tarpaulin, he recognized the Vietnamese driver, a friend of the master sergeant in charge of base supply. Beneath the truck's tarp were supplies intended for army personnel, and in the sergeant's stateside bank account were thousands of dollars he had made selling them.

Caffey spoke into his friend's silence. "I thought we come over here to fight communism, but looks like the government down here is as bad as the one up in Hanoi."

"From what I've seen," Cassidy turned back to Caffey, "most of these people would just as soon we stay at home. The only reason they tolerate us is because of the goodies we keep shipping over here and the money they make on the black market."

"Yeah, maybe so, but we still got a job to do." Caffey's voice had lost some of its enthusiasm. "I think a medic they call 'Boxie' might be going along with us."

"Boxie?"

"Yeah," Caffey answered, slapping the bolt of his M–16 open. "It's from the Vietnamese word *bac-si*. It means doctor."

"It's on for tomorrow, boys." Abe stood in the doorway, a grin spread across his long face.

"What's on?" Caffey asked, his face eager, the gun gripped tightly in his hands.

"We're going to a valley up north, a VC area. Supposed to verify their strength and location." Abe's expression looked as though they were going on some marvelous adventure, but his voice held a thin, nervous edge. "Sergeant Tree and Boxie are going with you guys, and Rufus and I get Lieutenant Hoa and Sergeant Bung. I think the VC might just as well surrender and get this war over, with us on the way."

"They're probably getting all the white flags ready right now," Cassidy muttered. Sitting on the edge of his bunk, he began sharpening his K-bar on an oiled whetstone.

Caffey, speechless at first, turned wide-eyed toward Cassidy. "This is it!"

TWELVE

NIGHTSHADE

★ ★ ★

At the sound of a bell, the H–34 leaped upward, the base disappearing in a swirling cloud of dust. Cassidy sat in the helicopter doorway, his legs dangling over the edge. Next to him Sergeant Tree studied his map. Behind Cassidy sat Boxie. He would not only be the medic but would also maintain the radio on this mission. Caffey sat on the canvas seat next to the door. Giving Cassidy a thumbs-up sign, he tucked his soft camouflage hat into his shirt so it wouldn't be lost in the prop wash when they hit the ground.

Cassidy leaned back on his pack, easing the weight, enjoying the coolness as the helicopter gained altitude. The roar of the engine washed over them, isolating each man with his own thoughts. Cassidy pictured Linda's face framed by the soft sweep of her hair, felt the touch of her lips on his, smelled the fragrance of her skin. Then he thought of his family, gathered around the breakfast table on Saturday morning. . . .

Pushing memories aside, Cassidy leaned over the edge of the door. Far below, the last rays of sunlight slanted across the canopy of green-black jungle. The bell rang again, telling him they were passing over the four-mile valley that would be their operational area. He gazed down, wondering what waited for them below the treetops on the shadowy jungle floor. As they made a long pass to the north, waiting for the cover of total darkness, he saw a village in flames.

Suddenly the chopper banked left, dropping with a heart-stopping rush toward the jungle. Cassidy checked his rifle, left hand tapping the magazine securely into place, then slipping forward to grasp the hand guard. He pulled back the bolt, made certain a round fed into the chamber, slammed it home, and checked the safety one final time.

Zipping along just above the treetops, the chopper started vibrating as though it would shake apart, then dropped straight down. Cassidy watched the long grass flattening under the prop wash. He flicked the weapon's safety to the automatic fire position. Then he leaped into the violent wind and rippling grass, followed by the other three men. Before the last man's feet touched the ground, the H–34 catapulted upward and roared away over the treetops.

Cassidy sprinted across the landing zone five yards ahead of Caffey and the two Vietnamese. Gathering at the tree line, the men held to one another's packs and moved ten yards into the complete blackness of the jungle.

"Two hours before we can make radio contact," Cassidy whispered, knowing this was the critical time. If their team should come under fire now, the base could do nothing to help them.

Caffey, his voice strained and hoarse, pushed close

to his longtime friend. "You see any sign of the VC?"

Knowing that the question would have already been answered by AK–47 fire if the enemy had been nearby, Cassidy ignored it. He opened his compass with a faint click, passing his forefinger around the edge of its luminous dial, then stopped to indicate their line of march. Cassidy moved off into the thick jungle, the other three holding on to the pack of the man in front of him. Stopping every few minutes to listen, they soon came upon a small stream.

This is a break, Cassidy thought, *no more fighting through vines and undergrowth.* "We'll follow it uphill, away from the LZ," he whispered and turned into the stream bed.

Suddenly a shot rang out. All four men instinctively dove for cover. Then they sat up and opened their compasses. The sound came from the direction of the LZ.

"Didn't take them long," Caffey said, speaking the thoughts of the other men.

Back into the stream, they made better time now, putting distance between them and the rifle fire from the LZ. Ten minutes later Cassidy stepped out of the stream, moving twenty yards into the jungle. "We'll spend the night here." He took his pack off, pulling out the ground sheet and HT–1 radio. "Everybody know the rendezvous point in case we get separated in a fire fight during the night?" The three men indicated they did.

Sporadic firing suddenly broke out. All four men opened their compasses as though on order. It came from the direction of the LZ, a VC trick to get return fire so their position would be revealed. The men applied mosquito repellent, then lay on their backs, rifles across their stomachs, right hands on the stocks.

Hearing the distant drone of the C–47, which acted as their base, Cassidy crawled beneath his ground cover. He attached the earplug, turned the radio on, and pushed the transmit button three times, making sure he had contact before he spoke a word.

"Nightshade, this is Falcon Two. Do you have traffic? Over." The muffled voice sounded like a shout in the night silence.

Cupping his hands around the mouthpiece, Cassidy spoke in a low, distinct voice. "This is Nightshade. Affirmative. Do you read me?"

"This is Falcon Two. Read you five-by. Send your message. Over."

Cassidy transmitted their location and intended route for the next day. "How copy? Over."

"This is Falcon Two. I read back . . ."

No mistakes. I don't have to repeat it, Cassidy thought gratefully.

"If message correct and you have no further transmission, acknowledge by pushing button once."

Cassidy pushed the transmission button, letting his breath out softly.

"Roger. Understand no further transmission. Out."

Stowing the radio in his pack, Cassidy lay on his back again, M–16 at the ready. He listened to the soft breathing of the men forming the other three corners of a rough square. Out in the thick darkness, a predator crept through the jungle; mosquitoes whined around his face. Knowing the predawn quiet as the night animals found their lairs would awaken him, he applied mosquito repellent, let his mind relax, and drifted into sleep.

★ ★ ★

First light . . . a thin pink glow barely filtering

down through the high canopy. Cassidy sat up stiffly, easing his pack around in front of him. Stowing the ground sheet, he took a small plastic bag of precooked rice from a side pocket of the pack, added water from his canteen, sugar and chunks of dried pineapple, then replaced it in the pocket. He listened to the rising chorus of birds and squirrels, to the other men stirring, getting ready to face the heat, thirst, snakes, and the wraithlike, black-clad enemies who waited for them out in the jungle.

"Maybe we lost them," Caffey said hopefully, but his words died away into a mumble.

"Maybe the sun will go back down in the east." Cassidy immediately put an end to any sense of false confidence, knowing it could be fatal. He slipped his arms into the shoulder straps of the pack and stood up.

In the dimness, Cassidy motioned them closer, four faces only inches apart as he spoke. "They'll expect us to crisscross the valley on our way south. The ambushes will be set up for that, so we'll head due south. Boxie. . . ?"

"I agree."

"Good. We'll make our first crossover a few miles down the valley."

Cassidy moved them out, following Boxie, who took the point, with Caffey next, and Sergeant Tree acting as rear guard. Vines grabbed at Cassidy's arms and legs; thorns raked his skin. In minutes he was soaked with sweat; salt burned his eyes; humidity was a hot, wet blanket smothering him. In an hour he called a break, the men fanning out in a defensive perimeter.

Taking out his plastic breakfast bag, Cassidy squeezed globs of the sweet rice and pineapple mixture into his mouth. Three swallows of water, a five-minute rest, and he signaled the men to resume the march. Three steps . . . *Bang!*

Cassidy whirled around, down on one knee, his heart beating against his rib cage, straining to see through the dense vegetation. He noticed a nervous grin on Boxie's face. The shot had seemed close but was twenty minutes on their back trail.

Cassidy headed them south again, fighting the heat, thorns, and vines, and the exhaustion that was dragging against them heavier than any of the vines. Breaks for salt tablets and water came every thirty minutes now. After each one that same single, eerie rifle shot sounded behind them, keeping the ambushers ahead advised of their progress.

By midafternoon the canteens were empty. After a few mouthfuls of rice, Cassidy checked his map. "There's a stream about a half mile southwest."

"Perfect place for the ambush." Boxie's soft voice carried little farther than the area the four men occupied.

Cassidy nodded and started them toward the stream. The twin burdens of fatigue and thirst added their own special torture to the threat of enemy ambush. Abruptly the ground dropped away. Tall ferns grew in abundance. The stream was near. The men could smell the water. All three sat down, backs against tree trunks, making themselves comfortable.

Relief flooded over Cassidy. He knew that after the endless hours of training, Caffey would remember, but less-experienced Vietnamese soldiers would have headed straight for the water. After a fifteen-minute wait, it happened: the sound of chopping from the direction of the stream, a sharp cry of pain, men muttering among themselves, settling in for the ambush.

Ten minutes later, Boxie crawled over to the edge of the bank, standing slowly until he could see over the ferns, then gazed downstream. Turning back toward Cassidy, he held up six fingers. After checking upstream, he held up four fingers.

Cassidy nodded, his throat dry, his heart racing, pounding against his rib cage. He moved slowly, carefully, over to the bank next to Boxie. Peering over the tops of the ferns, he surveyed the ambush. Two light machine guns in each brush-screened emplacement. All ten men armed with AK–47s.

Pulling the pin on a grenade, Cassidy motioned for Boxie to fill his canteen and cross to the sandbar on the opposite side of the stream. Flicking his safety to automatic fire, Boxie held his M–16 in one hand, letting the water run into the neck of the canteen so it wouldn't make a gurgling noise. Then he glanced both ways and carefully made his way across the shallow stream. Looking not at the enemy but at the stream bed, he stepped only on flat rocks—muddy water would flow past the men downstream, alerting them. Once across, he disappeared into the undergrowth.

Cassidy let his breath out slowly. He knew that Boxie would move downstream to a position where he could bring fire on the six VC. Caffey was suddenly crouched next to him. *Good job. Didn't hear him coming.* Handing the grenade to Caffey, Cassidy filled his canteen, crossed the stream, and moved upstream, taking cover opposite the other machine-gun nest.

Pushing a thick fern aside, Cassidy gazed at the four slender men down below him. Clad in shapeless black shirts and trousers, they looked like fourteen-year-olds playing soldier. Then he focused on the machine gun and the AK–47s. He knew he could take them out if anything went wrong with the crossing

191

and that Boxie could do the same with their buddies downstream. But that would bring a hundred, maybe two hundred of their fellows racing through the jungle toward them.

Ten minutes later, Cassidy joined the other three men as they moved uphill away from the stream. At the top they turned south for fifteen minutes, then settled into the underbrush for a break. Bird calls and the drone of insects were the only sounds.

"The enemy positions must be a little farther south." Cassidy's whisper sounded like a shout to him. He glanced at the sun, dropping toward the mountains in the west. "We'll rest a few minutes, then slip through them before dark and call a chopper in for first light."

Sergeant Tree and Boxie nodded. Swallowing two salt tablets with water from his canteen, Caffey stared at Cassidy, his face pale beneath the sweat and grime.

Cassidy knew it would only be a matter of time until someone saw their footprints on the sandbar at the crossing. Then they would make a sweep through the jungle looking for them. He lay back, staring at the slanting lavender light breaking on the leaves far above. Remembering the classes on torture, he knew he would never allow himself to be taken alive.

★ ★ ★

On the move again, the men followed in single file, picking each step, ears and eyes straining to pick up any sign of the VC. Bird calls and the dull droning of insects were all around. Their legs grew heavy, sweat burned their eyes, soaking through clothing.

Then came the murmur of voices. Cassidy pushed undergrowth aside and saw a small clearing with a shelter made of brush. In front of it three men sat cleaning their weapons. Signaling behind him, he moved off, circling to the left, then avoiding two more hooches set in small clearings. Woodsmoke now filled the air. Tree cuttings lay all around them as they moved south.

Stepping past a large tree trunk, Cassidy saw a rifle barrel swinging around toward him. As he spun around behind the tree, a burst of automatic rifle fire ripped chunks of bark loose. All four men cut loose with their M–16s, crouching low, running backward, laying down a wall of fire in the direction of the enemy. Bullets were clipping leaves and tree branches off all around them.

Cassidy soon realized they were on the edge of the enemy encampment. He jerked an empty clip out, slammed a full one home, and fired controlled, short bursts at dark forms barely visible through the thick jungle. The enemy firing grew sporadic as they moved farther south, but he knew others would be joining them. *Maybe most of them are laid up in ambushes up north. Maybe they don't know we've slipped by them yet. Maybe . . .*

Realizing that the VC would soon organize a sweep up from the south, forming a pincers movement with the forces north of them, he made a decision that went against all his training.

"We've got to get past them to the south before they can organize." The three men crouched next to him in the lee of a giant tree. Underbrush hid them on all sides. He pointed to a trail twenty feet away.

"No trails." Boxie knew from experience that to use the VC trails meant almost certain ambush.

Sergeant Tree, his dark face a mask of fatigue and fear, gazed directly into Cassidy's eyes. "Sure death."

"It's sure death if we don't get past the VC before

193

they form a sweeping movement. They'll think they've got plenty of time, that we're going to be moving through the thick brush." Cassidy glanced again at the brightness of the trail. He felt naked just thinking about stepping out of cover onto it. "I believe they'll stay clear of the trail thinking we won't be anywhere near it."

"It's the only chance we've got," Caffey admitted, glancing back toward the north.

Boxie and Tree glanced at each other, then at the trail. Each man looked at Cassidy and nodded his head in turn.

Cassidy slammed a fresh clip home, forced a smile toward the three men, and said, "Ten minutes at a fast pace ought to put us past them."

Boxie nodded his agreement.

Taking a deep breath, Cassidy rose quickly, stepped out of their shadowy cover, and sprinted south. He cut his speed when he was twenty-five yards ahead of the others, knowing that if the VC hit him the other three would get enough warning to have a fighting chance. His world became a blurred vision of green flashing past him; the slanting sunlight shattered in the crowns of the trees; blood pounded in his ears. Any moment he expected to be torn by automatic rifle fire.

Run the race. Cassidy thought at first that someone had spoken to him. He looked around as he ran, seeing only the three men still behind him. *"I have fought a good fight. I have finished my course. . . ."* The words stuck in his mind. *But I don't even know why I'm fighting . . . or what my course is.* He shoved the thoughts out of his mind and ran, thinking now only of survival.

Cassidy glanced down at his watch. The ten minutes had passed. Waving the others to a halt, he led them a hundred yards out into the jungle. Then they headed back toward the south, passing quietly through a maze of trails leading to innumerable shelters, each with a charcoal fire. Men clad in black sat around at their leisure, cooking, eating, talking in a high, strange tongue.

Calling a break in a dense thicket, Cassidy spoke in a barely audible voice, the faces of the three men inches from his own. "They think we're still north of them. Either that or they haven't heard about the fire fight yet."

"They think nobody stupid enough to run on trail in open daylight." Boxie gave him a thin-lipped smile, showing the relief he felt.

Cassidy nodded agreement, then glanced at the red glow in the western sky. "It'll be dark in thirty minutes. We'll move south twenty more minutes. I hope we clear the encampment by that time."

"Regiment strength here, maybe more." Boxie had made a rough count of the enemy's strength as the team moved through their positions.

"Next scheduled contact is at 2100 hours. They've got to get us out of here at first light." Cassidy took out his map and compass, then took a quick fix on the highest peak. "I hope they can spot an LZ for us from the air."

The men moved south, found thick cover in the failing light, and settled in for the night. At dusk they saw firelight flickering out in the jungle. Muted voices carried on the damp air. Then came the sound of men on the hunt growing closer and the clank of weapons.

Cassidy knew the VC were moving into position, blocking all the trails and streams. In the morning they would make their sweep, closing the circle on the four men, as soon as the sun sought them out. *It's gonna be real close.*

At 2100 Cassidy motioned the three men closer, blocking sound with their bodies as he turned the radio on.

"Nightshade, this is Falcon Two. Over."

"This is Nightshade. How copy? Over."

"This is Falcon Two. Read you five-by."

Again Cassidy spoke slowly and distinctly, afraid of giving away their position if he had to repeat the message. "This is Nightshade. Fire fight. Zero friendly killed. Zero wounded. Evading two or more companies Victor Charlie. All around us. Vital. Repeat, vital. Send chopper before first light to area four-two-three-niner for code blue pickup. Read back after vital."

"This is Falcon Two. Read back: Send chopper . . . if affirmative push button once. Over."

Cassidy complied, thinking that the conversation would never end.

"Roger, Nightshade. Wait one. Break . . . Ops Center has monitored request and will comply. Over."

Letting his breath out slowly, Cassidy pushed the button a final time.

"Roger, Nightshade. See you at first light with hot coffee. Over."

Cassidy stowed the radio, moved his pack behind him, and tapped the bottom of his clip to make certain it was secure. As the men settled down about him for the coming night, he rested his rifle on his stomach. Occasionally murmuring voices would awaken him from a fitful drowse. *Getting ready to nail us in the morning. They don't give up.*

★ ★ ★

It was still dark when Cassidy woke up. With a

touch the other men were roused, and they immediately pushed back into the jungle. Vines clutched at them, thorns ripped exposed flesh. *Must move quietly. Plenty of time.* They came to a brighter spot through the trees and sat down just inside the tree line. Cassidy turned on the radio.

"Nightshade, this is White Wolf. Over."

They made it! A quarter mile west of our position. Relief flooded through Cassidy. "This is Nightshade. Fly due south. When I say mark, take heading two six zero. Out."

"Roger, Nightshade."

A few shots rang out in the vicinity of the helicopter. Cassidy set his compass at eighty degrees, waited until the chopper was on line, then said, "White Wolf, mark."

"Roger, Nightshade. Turning two six zero. Out."

Cassidy listened to the sound of the Huey getting closer. He could hear the blades slapping the air, the roar of the engine. Closer. . . . "Now!"

The chopper flew over them at five hundred feet, then disappeared above the canopy, its sound fading away. Knowing their exact location, the pilot headed south looking for an area open enough to pick them up.

Cassidy hung the radio over his shoulder, the earplug still in place, leading back into the thick underbrush, circling the first clearing. Yellow light splashed down through the trees. Sounds of voices, searching behind and on both flanks, were getting closer. A second helicopter, acting as decoy, roared over the jungle, heading northwest, then began a tight circle one mile away as though waiting to pick up the men on the ground.

A dark blur on Cassidy's left broke in a small clearing—two men in black. Whirling and dropping to one knee, he ripped off three quick bursts. The men crumpled. Pulling the spent clip out, he slammed a fresh one home and rushed on through the brush. There was no reason left for caution now.

As Cassidy pushed south, the radio exploded in his ear, White Wolf giving the team's exact location and the coordinates for an LZ due south of them. Shouts came from off to their right.

"This is White Wolf. Five bandits on trail ten yards west."

Cassidy stopped, holding up five fingers. All four men raked the jungle to their right with quick bursts, slapped fresh clips in, and continued their race south.

A sudden brightness brought Cassidy to a halt. *The LZ! Can't bring the chopper in without checking the perimeter.* He waved Sergeant Tree and Boxie to the left, Caffey to the right. They would take up the other three points of the compass around the LZ, facing toward the jungle.

Cassidy spotted a green speck in the southwestern sky. He pulled a thick mirror with a peephole in its center out of his pocket. Checking the sun's angle, he aimed it at the treetops across the clearing and sighted in. The speck was a tiny helicopter now. He aimed the reflected sunlight toward the helicopter, then wiggled it back and forth.

"This is White Wolf. See your signal."

Cassidy heard the drone of the engine. Off to his right, Caffey cut loose on automatic fire.

"This is White Wolf. We're coming in."

Cassidy watched the chopper drop toward the clearing, its engine roaring, the prop blast flattening the grass. On both flanks and directly across from him, the other three men raced toward the waiting safety of the helicopter.

Automatic rifle fire burst from behind Cassidy and bullets snicked past his head. He turned deliberately and emptied a full clip toward the sounds, jerked it out, slapped in another, and fired another full clip. Spinning around he saw the three other men clambering aboard the helicopter.

Holding his rifle and radio in front of him, Cassidy sprinted across the clearing. Shots rang out behind him. He saw grimy, strained faces urging him on, arms reaching out for him. Bullets whined past his ears. At six feet he launched his weapon and radio . . . a half second later he dove headfirst into the open door . . . hands grabbed him, pulling him to safety . . . the chopper leaped skyward, a few rounds spanging against the airframe.

Caffey grabbed Cassidy in a bear hug, clapping him on the back. Rolling over, Cassidy sat up, grinning back at the other three grimy, grinning faces. Glancing down, he saw the clearing growing smaller, a few tiny men emerging from the jungle, then it disappeared in the vast green canopy. He gazed at the blue sky, felt the cool air on his face.

PART FOUR

★ ★ ★

CLOSE TO THE HEART

THIRTEEN

LINDA IN WHITE

★ ★ ★

"It wasn't so bad. Abe's team caught it worse than we did." Cassidy sat next to Linda at the little food stand on the beach. "They lost a Vietnamese scout."

Linda, pulling her tiger-striped fatigue shirt close to her neck, shivered slightly in spite of the afternoon warmth. "I can't bear to think of going out into those jungles. Some of the boys told me stories about the awful things the Vietcong do to the soldiers they capture."

Cassidy took a swallow of Coke from his moisture-beaded bottle. "You've been talking with the boys, have you?" He showed his teeth. "I leave for two or three days and you're already getting together *with the boys*."

"Well, I guess that part's wrong. Actually, I was over at the officer's club, so I guess you'd say I got together with *the men*." She watched Cassidy's eyes narrow, then smiling, leaned over and kissed him on the cheek.

"Yeah, you probably wouldn't like it over at the EM Club." Cassidy felt the spark of anger fade away. "Cookies and milk mostly. They promised us if we're

203

good, though, they'll send out for some Kool-Aid."

Linda laughed, combed her hair back from her face with her fingers, and said, "I really like you, Cassidy. It makes me feel . . . nice being around you."

"Like?" Cassidy stared directly into Linda's eyes. "Did you say *like*?"

"Sure. What's wrong with that?"

"Last week the word was *love*."

Linda looked away toward the beach. Sunlight shattered on the wind-rippled sea. "So . . ."

"Big difference, Linda," Cassidy replied, his stomach feeling as though he had swallowed a thin sliver of ice. "Like . . . love. Kind of like dead . . . not dead. Big difference."

"Oh, Cassidy!" Linda said, shaking her head slowly. She glanced at him, then stared down at her Coke. "Ten thousand miles from home, strolling together on the beach, in the moonlight . . . people say all kinds of things."

"I'm not interested in all the things *people* say, Linda." Cassidy realized then he should have kept his mouth shut, but he felt somehow betrayed, although no promises had been made. "I'm talking about what *you* said!"

"Would you stop shouting . . . please?"

"I'm not shouting!" Cassidy yelled.

Linda spun around on her stool. "I don't want to have this conversation."

Cassidy stepped around in front of her. "You always get everything you want?"

"You're acting like a child!" She turned away from him, knocking her Coke bottle over, spilling it on the counter. The little woman bending over the stove gave her a blank look as though this kind of thing happened all the time.

"Now who's shouting?"

"Look what you made me do!" Linda slid off the stool, walking rapidly across the road toward the beach.

Catching up to her, Cassidy said, "Hold on a minute!" He took her arm.

"Let me go!" She pulled at his wrist with her free hand. "You're hurting me!"

Letting her arm go, Cassidy watched her rub it, then turn and stare out at a sailing ship, barely visible on the glittering surface of the sea.

"I thought you were a nice person." Linda's voice carried a sharp edge beneath the softness.

Cassidy saw no point in replying. Above him the lofty palm fronds rattled in the breeze. A truck roared past on the road behind him.

After a few seconds, Linda glanced at him, then walked toward the waves breaking on the shore. Cassidy stood his ground beneath the palm trees. A few yards down the beach Linda turned and gazed back at him. She looked again at the sea, then slowly walked back toward him, a sheepish grin on her face.

"How did that all start?"

Cassidy shrugged. "Beats me."

Stepping close to him, she slipped her forefinger inside his hand and gazed into his eyes, a smile beginning at the corners of her red lips. "I'm sorry . . . if you are."

Cassidy nodded. He found it difficult to hold on to his anger as she pressed against him.

Slipping her arms around his waist, Linda pressed her face against his chest. "I really do enjoy being with you, Cassidy. Is it all right to say that?"

"Why not?"

Placing her hands on his shoulders, she raised up and kissed him on the mouth, one hand moving across to the back of his neck, fingers entwining in his hair.

Cassidy returned her kiss, feeling the last of his anger melt away in the warmth and the softness of her lips. He forgot the heat and the thirst and the men in black who had tried their best to kill him, losing himself in Linda's embrace.

Suddenly she pulled free. "I don't think I can do this."

"Do what?" Cassidy found himself at a complete loss as to what was going on in her mind. "I don't understand what's happening with you. One minute you're all hugs and kisses, and the next you're acting like a stranger."

Linda's eyes grew bright with tears. She brushed at them with the backs of her hands. "I . . . I don't want to care this much about you. I don't!"

Again Cassidy had no idea how to respond to Linda's mercurial mood changes.

Linda crossed her arms defensively. "I have a few drinks at the Officer's Club to keep from worrying myself sick about you, and you make a big deal out of it."

"Okay. Let's just forget it."

"I don't know if I could go through another night with you out there . . . not knowing whether I'd ever . . ." Linda stifled a sob. "I've never been around anything like this before. You could get killed out there."

Linda's words forced Cassidy to confront the one thing none of the team members talked about. "Not much chance," he lied. "We can have the choppers in to lift us out of there in minutes when it gets too hot."

"Maybe it's because you're from the south."

"What's that got to do with anything?"

"You're just so . . . provincial."

"You want to explain that?"

"I've lived in Washington, and even in Paris and Madrid when my father was stationed there with the state department," Linda stated with emphasis on Paris and Madrid, "and you've lived all your life in South Louisiana."

"Don't forget my four years in Sweetwater, Mississippi." Cassidy fought to keep down his anger. "You certainly couldn't call a man from a metropolis like that provincial."

Linda ignored his comment. She unfolded her arms, wrinkling the hem of her shirt through her fingers. "And then you're getting upset just because I went out—I mean, because I went to the Officer's Club."

"You already said that . . . so you wouldn't have to worry about me, remember?" Cassidy had not missed Linda's slip of the tongue, but he kept silent as she continued her explanation.

"Why, President Kennedy had to activate the National Guard just to get James Meredith enrolled at Ole Miss." She gave a little victory nod with her head.

"Yeah, maybe you're right," Cassidy agreed with a shrug. "I tried my best to keep that boy out, but them confounded Yankees just wouldn't let well enough alone."

Linda forced a frown on her face, then almost immediately broke into laughter. "You see, I can't stay mad at you." She spun around, facing away from him. "But I *have* to stay mad at you. It just won't work between us."

"What's the problem now? Is it because you're Episcopalian and I'm an optimist?"

Linda turned around, a puzzled look on her face. "But I'm not an Episco—very funny, Cassidy." She threw herself into his arms, holding him tightly.

Cassidy held her close, feeling her breath against

his neck. The fragrance of her perfume reminded him of home and the springtime girls at LSU smelling like flowers.

"Oh, I don't know what I mean anymore. I don't know what to do anymore."

"Then do nothing."

Linda leaned back, gazing upward at him, a question in her eyes. "Nothing?"

"Well, maybe one thing."

"What's that?"

Cassidy smiled. "You can keep your arms around me for a while . . . that is, if you've got nothing better to do."

Linda pressed close to him again, a deep sigh escaping her lips, then dying as the sea breeze took it away.

Cassidy held her tight, feeling her so close, but somehow he felt that it was all unreal . . . that she was even then slipping away from him.

★ ★ ★

"The ARVN troops need to hit them now!" Abe paced back and forth in his room, his eyes on Washburn sprawled on the bunk, the soles of his big boots flat against the blanket. "Before they can get out of there."

"You think you know more than the President?"

Abe stopped pacing, then glanced over at Caffey, sitting on the edge of his mattress reading his Bible. "Is there something I'm missing here?"

Grinning, Cassidy said, "I think Rufus's keen political insight is too much for you, Abe." He enjoyed the exchanges between Abe and Rufus, two people from opposite ends of the country as well as the educational and political spectrums.

Washburn smirked, then rolled over into a sitting position, feet on the floor. "Yeah. You're missing the fact that you're not in charge of this war. The President is."

"We went in there and got solid numbers and positions on the VC, Rufus." Abe controlled his speech, although color had risen in his face. "Now the ARVN boys have already started broadcasting that they're going into that valley to clean out the VC. You know as well as I do that in two or three days, when they finally get their operation off the ground, all they'll find is some empty clearings and a few fish bones."

"So . . ."

"So you laid your life on the line just like the rest of us did." Abe's voice now rose in anger. "Doesn't it bother you that you did it for nothing?"

"Wudn't for nothing."

"What was it for, then?"

"My President and my country." Washburn stood up, stepping forward, his face only inches from Abe's.

Abe blew his breath out, shook his head in a gesture of futility at continuing the conversation. "Would you please elucidate, Professor Washburn?"

Washburn's eyes seemed to go out of focus, his lips moving soundlessly. Then he said, "College boy."

"Explain." Cassidy said, throwing a little gasoline on the fire. "He wants you to explain."

"Yeah, well, why didn't he say so, then?" Washburn grunted. "That's easy. If we don't fight 'em here, we'll be fighting 'em on the beaches of California."

Cassidy had heard the same sentence countless times. It had been the anthem of their classrooms.

Rubbing the back of his neck, Abe said, "You wanna know what I think, Rufus?"

"Not particularly."

"I think if they got one look at that bunch of weird-oes out in California, they'd hop in their little boats and head for home."

Washburn knotted his thick-fingered hands into fists. "You talk like a traitor," he said, then his eyes bulged as he struggled to think of a worse name. "Like a . . . a beatnik!"

Cassidy rubbed his chin. "Hmm . . . not a bad idea, Rufus. Why don't you grow a beard, Abe? Get some dark glasses."

"I'm not staying in the same room with a—" Washburn shoved Abe aside and stormed out of the room.

Giving Cassidy a blank look, Abe said, "I see this picture of Washburn and me . . . Germany 1942 . . . he's loading me on a train at gunpoint. See you fellas at chow." He turned and started to leave the room.

"Where you goin'?"

"Patch things up with him," Abe shrugged. "We've got a lot more missions ahead of us. Can't have a man mad at me when my life might depend on him some-day."

Caffey watched Abe leave, then returned to his Bible. "You know something?" He placed his finger on the page and turned to look at Cassidy.

"Not much." Cassidy lay down on his bunk, clasp-ing his hands behind his head. "I used to think I knew a few things, but I'm not so sure anymore."

Caffey continued, not allowing Cassidy to break his train of thought. "We could get killed over here."

"Now, *that* I know." Cassidy raised up on one el-bow, gazing at his friend. "That is *definitely* something I know."

Holding his Bible with both hands, Caffey said in a solemn voice, "I think I'm gonna get saved."

Cassidy sat up, a puzzled look on his face. "You mean just like that?"

"Yep." Caffey took his finger off the page and read, " 'Whosoever shall confess that Jesus is the Son of God, God dwelleth in him, and he in God.' That's right here in First John."

"You think it's that easy, Caffey?"

Caffey gazed directly at Cassidy, his eyes lighted with the knowledge of a sudden truth. "That's what the book says."

Cassidy nodded his agreement. "Yeah, I've read it."

"And look over here." Caffey turned the page and continued, "In the next chapter John says, 'These things have I written unto you that believe on the name of the Son of God; that ye may know that ye have eternal life, and that ye may believe on the name of the Son of God.' " He closed his Bible, holding it with both hands. "Would you listen to me, Cass?"

Cassidy nodded, too stunned by his friend's unusual behavior to speak.

Caffey took a deep breath. "I believe that Jesus is God's only son; that he came down to this earth as a little baby; that He lived a life without sin and died on the cross for me; that He rose again on the third day." A smile lighted his face as he continued. "I believe that His blood has washed away all my sins and that someday I'm going to live with Him in heaven."

Cassidy watched tears roll down his friend's broad, guileless face. He never remembered that happening in all the years he had known him.

"I ask you to come live in my heart, Jesus, and I promise that I'm going to live for you from now on." Caffey, unaware of his own tears, asked, "Do you think that's good enough, Cass?"

Cassidy felt his throat constricting as he answered.

"I think you did real good, Caffey."

"I'm not too good at saying things. I wanna make sure I said it right."

"You did just fine." Cassidy felt as though something had changed in the room. "You feel any different?"

Caffey took one hand from his Bible and rubbed the side of his face. "I don't know . . . maybe . . . yeah, something seems kinda different."

"What is it?"

Caffey smiled. His face seemed somehow younger. "I think I'm kinda sleepy."

"Sleepy?"

"Yeah." The smile got wider. "I ain't been sleeping much since we got over here. Worried about . . . gettin' killed, I reckon." He lay back on his bunk, pulling the pillow beneath his head. "I might take a little nap." In seconds he was snoring softly.

Cassidy gazed at his friend, sleeping peacefully, his Bible still clasped in his hands. He listened to the distant rumble of artillery fire off in the mountains.

★ ★ ★

Cassidy pushed a limb aside and peered into the clearing. An uneasy feeling began worrying around at the back of his mind as though trying to form itself into a thought. Eight missions had given him an instinctive sense of danger. He had a sudden urge to turn around and vanish back into the shadowy protection of the trees.

Half hidden in the lush green jungle foliage, the village stood sleepy and quiet in the hot afternoon sunshine. The place smelled of manure, rice, and fish cooking in a pungent sauce. The high, relentless drone of insects seemed louder in the open air than it had in the thick forest. From the riverbank at the base of a long, easy slope, he heard the sounds of human voices and the slapping of wet clothes on stones.

Signaling with his hand, Cassidy stepped out into the clearing. The other three team members emerged from the jungle like grimy, hollow-eyed predators, joining him as he made his way cautiously toward the hooches. Their white walls and red-tiled or gray tin roofs were in marked contrast to the thatched huts of most villages in the area. They spoke of permanence and . . .

That's it! They're protected by the VC! Cassidy glanced toward the river. Several women had left their clothes and were splashing across the shallow water toward the opposite bank. An icy vapor of fear enveloped his heart.

"It's a trap!" Cassidy turned toward the other team members, but the *thunk* of the first mortar round leaving its tube told him it was too late.

The four men sprinted toward the tree line on the opposite side of the village, but the VC had already begun walking the mortars in toward them. The first explosion showered dirt and limbs into the air thirty yards in front of them; the next three hit ten yards closer. Shrapnel filled the air, jagged chunks of hot metal, buzzing like angry hornets.

Cassidy rushed toward a nearby house with a metal roof. Diving against the base of a thick white wall, he jerked his pack off and dug the radio out. *Thunk, thunk, thunk. . . .* The hollow sounds of mortars firing were followed by a lethal whirring noise shortly before they crashed in on the village.

Small-arms fire cracked at them from the edge of the jungle they had just left. Staring at the lights winking from rifle barrels in the shadows, Cassidy called for covering fire. Caffey, Boxie, and Sergeant Tree, sprawled next to hooches, laid down a wall of fire at the trees with their M–16s.

Shouting into the headset, Cassidy got base on the radio, giving their position and requesting immediate pickup. "Sounds like at least two companies out there." He noticed a clearing across the river, telling the voice on the radio that they would head for it as soon as they heard the first chopper coming in.

Bullets hummed all around them now, tearing at the walls of the houses, ripping limbs and leaves loose in showers of ragged green fragments. Explosions rocked the ground as the mortars rained down steadily upon the village.

Cassidy shouldered his weapon and emptied a clip toward the tree line in three short bursts. He noticed Sergeant Tree lobbing grenades at the enemy positions with his grenade launcher. "That'll keep their heads down."

After what seemed like an eternity, Cassidy heard the dull, rhythmic thropping of helicopter blades. Looking above, he saw three birds flying low over the green canopy, their door gunners pouring fire from M–60 machine guns into the edge of the jungle. Two choppers began a tight circle above the village, firing at the enemy while the third one soared straight across the river, hovering above the LZ.

"Let's move out!" Cassidy leaped up, sprinting among the burning hooches toward the slope leading down to the river. Throwing himself behind the edge of the bank, he saw Caffey on a dead run, driving toward the river, Boxie and Sergeant Tree just ahead of him. Cassidy raked the jungle with bursts from his rifle, laying down covering fire for the three men. When the three men reached the other side of the river, he saw the chopper beyond them dropping like a stone toward the clearing, the door gunner urging the men on.

Cassidy emptied a full clip toward the jungle, then leaped down the bank and splashed out into the shallow water, racing toward the opposite bank, his heart pounding, blood rushing in his ears. Gaining the shore, he turned on all his speed, reached deep inside for every bit of strength, and flew through the tall grass. He saw Caffey clamber aboard, then turn and beckon toward him with outstretched arms.

Suddenly, the lethal rushing *whoosh* of a mortar filled the air. In a blaze of light, Cassidy felt himself hurtling through space. The sound of great bells rang in his head. Someone grabbed at him . . . he felt himself being lifted . . . then darkness shut out the sound . . . the light . . . and he felt nothing at all.

★ ★ ★

"Doc says I'll probably limp the rest of my life," Caffey said, "but at least I'll still *have* the rest of my life." He lay in a white room on a narrow hospital bed, his left leg encased in a cast from hip to ankle.

Abe sat on the edge of the bed, holding a two-pound Whitman Sampler box. "Here . . . there's all kinds of candy in this. You gotta like some of it."

Caffey took the box, tearing into it immediately. "Never met a piece of candy I didn't like." Without consulting the candy guide on the lid, he grabbed a piece, stared at it, then placed it carefully back in the box. Shoving the box toward Abe, he said, "Here, you take a piece."

Shaking his head, Abe smiled at Caffey. "What's wrong? You don't like that brand?"

"Just . . . don't feel like it now." He closed the box, placing it on the table next to his plastic water pitcher.

"They tell me you're getting a bronze star for going back after Cassidy."

Caffey shrugged. "Maybe. Whoever knows what the army's gonna do?" His face brightened. "One thing they told me for certain, though . . . I'm going home."

"Yeah," Abe said sadly. "How am I gonna handle Rufus without you and Cassidy?" His voice dropped to a whisper. "By the way, how's he doing?"

"Didn't you hear? He died last night."

Abe whirled around. "You big dummy! Don't sneak up on me like that."

Cassidy leaned against the doorframe, his right eye and the right side of his head swathed in bandages. He wore cloth slippers and a maroon bathrobe and held an aluminum cane in his right hand. "If you were a *real* Green Beret, you would have heard me coming."

"How you feelin', Cass? Couldn't get the doctor to tell me anything except you'd live."

Walking unsteadily over to a metal folding chair, Cassidy sat down. "The bells finally quit ringing after a couple of days, but somebody set a buzzer off inside my head this morning." He tugged at his unbandaged ear. "Easing up a little bit now."

Abe glanced at his watch and stood up. "I gotta get to a briefing. See you around, Caffey." He clasped Cassidy by the shoulder. "Silver star for you, partner."

When Abe disappeared down the hall, Cassidy asked, "What's he talking about?"

"That's the rumor." Caffey opened the box of candy and held it toward Cassidy. "They say you're getting the silver star for saving our hides down by the river."

Cassidy shook his head at the candy, then stared at the bulky cast. "Looks like I only saved part of *you*."

"Nah. I got enough leg there to lose a hunk and still have plenty left over."

"Thanks for coming back for me."

Caffey looked at the pale, drawn face of his friend, tears coming to his eyes and blurring his vision. "Too many years together to just let you lie there."

Cassidy blinked his eyes several times, then rubbed them with his fingertips as though trying to clear his vision. "Daddy told me to look out for you. I wasn't much good at it."

"You looked out for me since I was ten years old. Don't hurt for me to do *one* thing for you."

Tapping his rubber-tipped cane on the floor, Cassidy stared blankly out the window.

"You know the best thing you ever did for me, Cass?" Caffey watched him, silent, unmoving. "You took me to Sunday school all those years."

"You mean the times we skipped and went to Sitman's Drugstore for chocolate malts?" Cassidy nodded his head slowly, like an old man would. "Boy, what I wouldn't give for one of those tall, thick malts right now."

Thinking back to those years, Caffey smiled. "What I mean is, that's where I first found out about Jesus."

Cassidy's eyes slowly focused on the present time. "Oh. . . ." He stared at Caffey as though he had just noticed him for the first time. "Yeah . . . I remember those Bible stories the teacher used to read to us."

"You all right, Cass?"

"What. . . ? Oh, sure." He stood up slowly. "I'm kinda dizzy, that's all. First time out, I guess." Walking slowly toward the door, he said in a hoarse voice, "Think I'll get on back to the room. Feeling kinda weak."

Caffey watched his only real friend in the world

shuffle out of the room. He had wanted to ask him about his eye; would he see again? But the time didn't seem right. Opening the box of candy, Caffey stared at it for a few seconds, closed it, and put it away. Then he took his Bible from beneath his pillow, lay back, and began to read. *"The Spirit of the Lord is upon me, because he hath anointed me to preach the gospel to the poor; he hath sent me to heal the brokenhearted, to preach deliverance to the captives, and recovering of sight to the blind, to set at liberty them that are bruised. . . ."*

★ ★ ★

Cassidy lay on his bed and stared at the ceiling. Its flat white sameness was somehow reassuring to him. Since his injury, since that last battle that had ended his career as a Green Beret in the United States Army, he seemed to be stumbling around in a dream. Nothing he thought or said seemed to come out as it should have. He knew what he wanted to say and do, but the message somehow failed to reach his voice and his muscles.

"Cass . . ."

He turned and saw her, even though he thought at first she were only part of the dream. She wore a white dress and white shoes and looked as though she were part of the room.

Linda stood in the doorway, holding her white purse in front of her. "I heard about your injury and just wanted to come by to see you before I left." She glanced to her right. "Is it all right if I come in?"

Cassidy nodded his permission. He wanted to speak to her, but he couldn't hold on to the words blowing around inside his head like leaves in an autumn wind.

Linda motioned toward the hall with her hand, then walked over to the bed. A tall man in a tailored gray suit followed behind her. "How're you feeling?" she asked, pulling the man alongside the bed next to her.

"Just . . . fine." Cassidy had to search for the second word in his two-word sentence.

"I'm so glad!" She turned toward her companion. "Cassidy Temple, this is Ron Jacobs. Ronnie's an old family friend."

Cassidy noticed that the way Ronnie held Linda around the waist was unlike any old family friend he knew.

"Pleased to meet you, Cassidy." Ron held out his hand.

Cassidy thought his smile would look right at home on a campaign poster. He nodded and shook hands, unable to work up enough will to say anything.

Jacobs flashed teeth as white as Linda's purse. "I want you to know the folks back home appreciate what you fellows are doing over here. I can't wait to get back and tell them what a fine job our boys are doing."

"Ronnie's with the state department," Linda said by way of explanation. "Daddy hired him years ago as his assistant, and he's almost like family now."

Cassidy nodded again. Even in his condition, he could read the writing on the wall.

Linda fidgeted with her purse. "I guess we'd better be going. Daddy sent Ronnie to fetch me back home."

"That's right," Jacobs added. "He started watching the news reports and was afraid something might happen to his little girl."

"I told him there was no danger over here and—" Linda glanced at Cassidy's bandaged face and stopped short. "I mean unless you have to . . ."

Jacobs stepped in. "We'd better leave, Linda. I think Cassidy needs his rest."

Still gazing at Cassidy, Linda nodded. "I'd like a few words with Cass."

"Sure, we've got a little time left," Jacobs agreed readily, glancing at his watch.

"Alone, Ronnie."

"Oh . . . why, certainly." With a final admonition for Cassidy to keep up the good work, he left.

Linda sat on the edge of the bed, taking Cassidy's hand between both of hers. She traced the red line of a scar left by a thorn along his wrist. "I'm sorry things turned out this way, Cass. I really do care for you . . . a great deal."

It doesn't matter anymore, Cassidy thought. *It just doesn't matter.*

Leaning over, Linda kissed him on the cheek. "Oh, Cass, if only things had been different . . . if only we had—"

"Good-bye, Linda," Cassidy said flatly. He stared beyond her at the glare of the window.

"But, Cass, if you only knew—"

Cassidy placed his fingertips against her mouth, stopping her in midsentence.

She released his hand slowly, stood up, and walked across the room and out the door. Her high heels made a hollow clicking sound on the tiled floor of the hallway.

Cassidy suddenly realized that he had known all along he couldn't hold her, that it was just a question of time before she laid him aside like the latest fad or fashion. And it didn't matter anymore. The war didn't matter. Had it ever really mattered? And Ginger and Kay and all the others . . . most of the time he had treated them with such casual, trifling unconcern. Had he ever truly cared about any of them . . . at all?

FOURTEEN

ROCK OF AGES AND BLACKBERRY PIE

★ ★ ★

"Look at those two." Glancing out the kitchen window into the shady backyard, Catherine took a plate from the soapy water, rinsed it, and handed it to Sharon. "Like two peas in a pod. Taylor looks more like Cassidy than he does Jessie or Austin, except for the hair, of course."

Sharon took the plate and began drying it. "I ran across a snapshot of Cassidy when I was looking through one of our old family albums the other day. If he'd had dark hair, I wouldn't have known him from Taylor."

Catherine watched Cassidy lift his nephew up on his shoulders, running around and around the fountain, winter leaves floating in its dark water. She could hear Taylor's shrill giggles coming faintly through the closed windows. "It's hard to believe he'll be five in April. Seems like only last year we were all together at the hospital waiting for him to be born."

The sound of cheering erupted from the living

room. "Sounds like LSU's ahead in the Cotton Bowl. You think they can beat Texas, Mama?"

Gazing at her son and grandson out in the backyard, Catherine shrugged. "I haven't kept up with them since Dalton played." She smiled at Sharon. "I'm fortunate there's one more in the family who doesn't care much for football, or I'd be doing these dishes by myself."

A shadow flickered in Sharon's warm brown eyes as she turned toward Catherine. "You think Cass is all right?"

"Well, I'd feel better if we knew whether he's going to recover vision in that right eye. All the doctor says is time will tell." Catherine scrubbed an especially stubborn stain with a Brillo pad. "But he's enrolled in LSU for the spring semester. That's an encouraging sign."

Sharon glanced out the window. Cassidy sat in a wrought-iron chair on the brick patio telling Taylor a story. The child seemed transfixed as he sat on his uncle's knee. "He's so quiet. Sometimes I hardly know he's my brother."

"Lane was a lot like that when he got home from the South Pacific." Memories of those long-ago years rushed at Catherine. Meeting Lane at the train station when Cassidy was only three years old. Waiting for him alone in New Orleans when he returned from Korea, still recovering from his wounds, walking like an old man. "He'll pull out of it."

Sharon started as another cheer arose from the living room. "I think he looks kind of dashing with that black eye patch, though. Reminds me of a swashbuckler from the old black-and-white movies."

Catherine frowned her disapproval. "I just wish his eye would get well so he could take the patch off."

"Dalton sure seems happy," Sharon said. "I'm so glad he married Justine. He couldn't have a better wife if I'd picked her myself."

Nodding agreement, Catherine added, "And he's doing so well coaching at LSU. I think he likes it even better than when he was a player."

"Looks like your little flock's finally settling down, Mama," Sharon said. She watched Cassidy and Taylor tossing a football around on the frost-burned grass beyond the patio. "Even your youngest and wildest."

Catherine sighed. "I don't know, baby. Cass still seems . . . restless, unsatisfied. I just hope he buckles down and studies when school starts."

"I think he will. He could always make good grades whenever he tried." Sharon pushed a wisp of hair back from her face with the back of her hand. "But he always acted like being smart was something to be ashamed of. Maybe he's grown up enough now to use his mind instead of trying to hide it."

"I still have my doubts that he's ready to settle down."

"You said the same thing about Jessie," Sharon reminded her mother, "and look at her. Austin, Taylor, and another baby due in May. You thought she'd never settle down, either, and now she's the 'Happy House-wife.' "

"Maybe you're right." Catherine gazed at her son and grandson still playing football. "But Cass has always been so different from the rest of you."

Sharon dried the last dish and stacked it on the counter. Then she kissed her mother on the cheek. "Who're you going to worry about when all of us finally get straightened out?"

Catherine smiled, looking out the kitchen window. "My grandchildren."

★ ★ ★

The little apartment above the garage in the backyard looked much the same as it did when the Temple family had moved into it seventeen years earlier. The kitchen held a small Frigidaire, a white enameled table with four straight-backed wooden chairs, and a four-burner gas stove that had to be lighted with a match.

The remainder of the room served as the living area and contained a striped sofa and matching chair with a scarred maple coffee table. A lamp with a picture of Roy Rogers rearing high on Trigger sat on the single end table. Several framed black-and-white prints of the Temple children in various stages of their childhood years hung on the walls. A Philco radio next to the lamp played at high volume.

Oh, the times they are a-changin' . . .

"Ain't that the truth." Cassidy lay on the couch, one leg draped over the back. He wore threadbare Levi's, white socks, and an LSU track sweat shirt. "Sometimes I think the world I grew up in never really existed."

Pointing toward her ears, Sharon said, "You mind if I turn the radio down a little?" Without waiting for an answer, she leaned over and flicked the knob.

Cassidy smiled. "Help yourself." He picked up a jelly jar with pictures of Elmer Fudd and Bugs Bunny on it from the floor next to the couch and took a long pull. "Whew! That'll put hair on your chest."

Sharon frowned, then stared directly at Cassidy's insipid smile. "It'll also put holes in your brain."

"Brain? What brain?" Bitterness lay just beneath Cassidy's attempt at humor. "I think what little I had ran out the hole that shrapnel punched in my head."

"You know something, maybe it's not the times that have changed at all."

"What's that supposed to mean?"

"Maybe it's just *you* who's done the changing."

"Could be." Cassidy stared out the window at the bleak, cold February day. Through the window, rain glistened on the black-green leaves of the live oak.

Sharon shivered slightly and pulled the sleeves of her bulky sweater down over her hands. "What happened to the brother I used to know, Cass? Always getting into something . . . usually something you shouldn't, but at least you were full of life." She gazed at his listless expression, the unkempt hair, a three-day stubble on his still-boyish face. "Now all you do is go to class and stay closed up back here like an old wolf."

"I like it back here." Cassidy glanced around the little apartment. "Remember what a mess it was in the mornings? Everybody getting ready for school. Me and Dalton hollering at you and Jessie to get out of the bathroom. Mama scrambling a dozen eggs at a time, trying to feed everybody."

Sharon's eyes glistened with the memory of those first years in Baton Rouge.

"And Daddy sitting at the table with his coffee, grinning at the whole thing like it was some kind of circus act." Cassidy took another swallow from the glass, then stared at Elmer Fudd holding his double-barreled shotgun. "Elmer oughta get him an M–16. Ol' Bugs wouldn't stand a chance then."

"Cass, you should try to forget about the things that happened in Vietnam."

"Why?" He rolled off the couch and walked into the kitchen. "We had a good time over there." Taking an ice tray from the refrigerator, he broke it open in the sink and tossed several cubes into his glass, then filled it from the square bottle on the table. "Three hots and a cot. What more does a man need? That and all the free ammunition you could ever want."

"Let's talk about it, then."

"Well, there was this little shack on the beach. An old lady ran it and she made the best food you—"

"I mean about the war," Sharon interrupted. "Maybe you need to get it out of your system."

"I don't think I can."

"Was it that awful?"

"No worse than any other war." He pulled out a chair and sat down at the table, staring at the amber liquid in his glass. "I just can't seem to remember much about the fire fights . . . and the mortars coming in on us. That part of it."

Sharon gave him a strange look, thinking she was about to learn something of war.

"All the noise . . . the small-arms fire, the grenades, and especially the mortars." Cassidy blinked and shook his head as though trying to bring his thoughts together. "It makes you kind of . . . goofy afterwards.

"Your skin feels thick, like there's not much feeling left in it. Things kind of blur together . . . no sharp outlines on anything." He took a sip from his glass. "Everything is just kind of . . . dead feeling. Nothing seems real anymore." His eyes sparked with sudden recognition. "People do strange things in combat. Maybe that's why. Nothing seems real anymore. It's like all the nerves in your body are beaten and dulled by the noise and shock waves . . . and thinking that any breath could be your last."

Sharon noticed the strange gleam in her brother's eyes. "Maybe you'd better not talk about it, Cass."

"No! I think I'm figuring something out here," he

said almost savagely. "It's like your own body is giving you anesthesia so you can go through it." He nodded his head slowly. "And then it wears off, and you wake up and can't remember very much about what happened. Everything is vague . . . and cloudy . . . almost like it never really happened at all. And the next day your memory slips a little and even more of it is gone."

Cassidy began nodding his head again. "I believe that's the answer. The mind puts some kind of shield up to protect you from things that are beyond bearing and then afterwards it takes the memory away . . . or most of it."

"That's pretty elegant stuff, Cass," Sharon said. He seldom showed his command of the language, and it always amazed Sharon when he let his guard down and spoke with such simple yet precise insight. "How are you doing in your journalism class?"

"Good." He saw the frown on his sister's face. "Okay. I'm making an *A* . . . and I guess I'm kind of enjoying it. The professor wants me to make it my major."

"Do it, then."

"Maybe I will." Cassidy got up and returned to the couch, sitting down on the arm next to Sharon's chair. "I had good friends over there. Guys I could depend on."

"You think Caffey's not your friend anymore since you're back home?"

"No. We've been through too much together. He'll always be my best friend." Cassidy looked off into the distance. "I'm glad he's happy now. Got his job back at the dairy science building out at LSU. Always puttering around his house, fixing something, making things look better. Got his life all straightened out."

"Good for him." Sharon shivered again.

Cassidy went to the kitchen, returned with a box of matches, and lit the small space heater in the living area. "That ought to warm you up." He put the matches away and returned to his seat on the arm of the couch.

Sharon stared at the blue-and-yellow flames in the grates of the heater. "Maybe if you'd been able to run track this year, things would have been better."

"Coach said I could get my scholarship back next year. All I have to do is run a nine-eight in the hundred."

"That ought to be easy enough. You ran better than that in high school, didn't you?"

"Got to be in shape, though. And the doctor says I can't start working out for at least six more months after the surgery next week."

Sharon glanced at her brother's black eye patch. "When your eye gets well, I think you ought to consider keeping the patch. Makes you look like a buccaneer."

"Yeah," Cassidy said, a trace of a smile flickering across his face. "I'm thinking about getting a cutlass and a parrot to go with it. What do you think?"

"The cutlass . . . maybe." Sharon tilted her head to one side, sizing him up. "I'd skip the parrot, though— too messy."

"How's the novel coming along?"

"I thought you'd never ask." Sharon's face glowed with suppressed excitement now that the subject had been brought up. "Just great!"

"What does that mean?"

Sharon stood up, doing a series of joyful pirouettes and leaps about the room, then she stopped in front of Cassidy, breathless with the exertion.

"The more you write, the goofier you get, Sharon."

She put her hands on Cassidy's shoulders, gazing into his eyes. "*Scribners* is publishing my novel in August!"

Cassidy looked stunned, then a smile spread across his face. "Published . . . and with Scribners! Man! That's Hemingway and Thomas Wolfe's publisher. They're the best!"

"I know!"

Cassidy stood up and hugged her, lifting her off the floor, spinning around. "This is great! My little sister's an honest-to-goodness novelist!"

At that moment Sharon thought that all the years, all the work, was worth it just to see the happiness in her brother's face. "It's a miracle, all right."

Setting her down, Cassidy held to his smile and said, "I'm so proud of you, Sharon."

Sharon felt her cheeks growing warm with embarrassment. "Thanks" was all she could think of to say.

★ ★ ★

"I just want to travel around for a while, Daddy." Cassidy sat in Lane's study, his duffel bag resting on the floor next to his chair. "See some of the country."

Lane gazed at his son, wearing sun-faded Levi's and an army fatigue shirt with the sleeves cut off. "I thought you might want to go to summer school. Catch up on the year you got behind when you were in the service."

Cassidy stared at the picture of Lane and his two friends standing on the beach at Guadalcanal. "I don't think I could handle sitting in a classroom all summer."

"Where you heading?"

Shrugging, Cassidy said, "I don't really know for

sure. Just that I'm not going west."

"Why's that?"

"Last time I headed west," he said with a wry smile, "I ended up in Vietnam."

Lane laughed. He had seen Cassidy's sense of humor returning in the past few weeks, and it gave him comfort that his son was on his way back. "You're kind of restless, are you?"

"Yeah, I guess so."

"I did something like you're doing once. It was the summer before my senior year in high school."

Cassidy's face lighted with interest. "Oh yeah? Where did you go?"

"West. I told Daddy I just had to see some of the country, so I hopped a freight train just outside of Sweetwater. Made it all the way to Amarillo, Texas."

Cassidy crossed his legs and sat back in his chair, enjoying a side of his father he had never seen before.

"I saw some of the country, all right. At first it was a real adventure. Places I'd never been, things I'd never seen, people different from anybody I'd ever known." Lane rubbed his chin between thumb and forefinger. "Then one August day I was hitchhiking just outside of Amarillo. Must have been a hundred and ten in the shade. I had a black eye and a sore jaw from a fellow who tried to rob me outside a barroom the night before."

"Outside a barroom?"

"Yep," Lane admitted with a nod. "Anyway, right out of the blue I thought about sitting down to supper at our farm in Sweetwater. I could taste the iced tea, the corn and squash and fried okra, and I could almost hear Mama singing 'Rock of Ages' while she was taking a blackberry pie out of the oven."

"And you headed for Mississippi," Cassidy finished the story for his father.

"And I headed for Mississippi," Lane repeated. "It was something I guess I needed to get out of my system."

"And I thought everything you ever did in your life was sensible."

"Not by a long shot." Lane gazed into Cassidy's intelligent, thoughtful eyes. "It took three years in the South Pacific to make me grow up some."

"Do you remember much about the battles you were in, Daddy?" Cassidy felt a slight burning in his palms, the way he sometimes had during a fire fight.

Lane's eyes focused on something in the air above Cassidy's head. "Not a whole lot. Everything was always kind of fuzzy after it was over." He nodded slowly. "Almost like it never happened . . . like a dream."

"I know what you mean."

"The things I do remember, especially after all these years, are so jumbled up in my mind they don't make much sense." Lane took a deep breath. "I suppose that's probably for the best. Friends . . . that's what I remember most."

Cassidy stood up. "Well, I guess I'd better get on the road. I've already told everybody good-bye."

"Okay." Lane got out of his chair.

With an awkward motion, Cassidy stuck out his hand. "Well, I'll see you, then."

As Lane reached for his hand, Cassidy stepped forward and put his arms around his father. Lane hugged him, patting him on the back.

"Don't stay gone too long, son."

"I won't."

As Cassidy turned to leave, Lane said, "Hold on a

minute." When Cassidy turned around, Lane tossed his car keys to him. "I think you'll like this better than the bus."

Cassidy looked stunned. "These are the keys to your Ford. You love that old car."

Lane nodded. "That's right."

"I'll take good care of it."

"I hope so. . . . It's yours now."

★ ★ ★

Heading east on Highway 190, Cassidy glanced to his right at the blue-green waters of the Gulf, sparkling in the June sunshine. Palm trees lined the beach. On the north side of the highway, long sloping lawns led up to white-columned homes with gazebos and gray-painted front porches.

The '39 Ford coupe purred like a sewing machine, its engine tuned to perfection, its shiny black paint and chrome gleaming as though he had just driven it out of the showroom. Cassidy remembered his father teaching him to drive in the "stick-shift" automobile; he called back memories of Saturday night dates and Sunday afternoon rides down the River Road during his high school and college days.

After passing the old Biloxi Lighthouse that split the highway north and south, Cassidy drove a few more miles and turned into a parking lot. Walking along a boardwalk toward the Gulf, he opened a glass door and entered a restaurant with pine flooring and wooden tables covered with red-and-white checked cloths.

"You're a little early, sugar. We don't start serving lunch for another fifteen minutes." Short and in her thirties with a round, sunny face, the waitress wore a black dress and a white name tag with "Odette" in red letters.

"Can I get a glass of tea while I wait?"

Odette gave him a coy smile. "You could probably get the title to my car if you hang around till I get off work."

Cassidy grinned back at her. "I already have a car, Odette, but I don't have any iced tea." He turned and walked toward one of the tables next to a long expanse of windows looking out onto the gentle swells of the Gulf.

Two minutes later Odette set a tall glass of tea in front of him and leaned against the table. "You some kind of soldier?" she asked, eyeing the twin chevrons on the sleeves of his fatigue shirt.

Cassidy spooned sugar into the tea and stirred it, ice making small music against the glass. "Not anymore."

"That where you got your eye hurt?"

Nodding, Cassidy gazed out at three pelicans flying low over the smooth surface of the water.

Odette proved to be persistent. "How'd it happen?"

"Vietnam."

"What's that?"

Cassidy turned toward her, saw that she was completely serious, and laughed. "It's a little country on the other side of the world."

"Are we fightin' a war over there or something?"

"If we're not," Cassidy answered, a grin still on his face, "somebody's sure wasting a lot of bullets."

"Probably ain't got no business being there in the first place." Odette plucked a pencil from behind her ear and flipped her ticket pad to an empty page. "Just like them federal troops didn't have no business being in Montgomery."

"You mean when people up there were attacking the Freedom Riders?" Cassidy grabbed a menu leaning against the napkin holder and flipped it open.

"Yeah. Governor Wallace knows how to run his state, but that Kennedy just won't let well enough alone." Odette shook her head sadly as though she could see the world she had grown up in passing slowly away. "He better keep them troops ready, too."

"Why's that?"

"Gonna be trouble this summer. They already startin' to act up over in Birmingham." She glanced over her shoulder toward the front door. "It's that Martin Luther King, you know. Always stirrin' things up."

"Sounds like something I'd like to see."

Odette gave him a skeptical frown. "Hey, you ain't one of them civil rights people, are you?"

Cassidy shook his head.

"Where you from?"

"I was born up in Sweetwater." Cassidy knew the method for putting him above suspicion. "Guess I'll have the fried shrimp and hush puppies."

Odette scribbled on her pad. "Oh well," she said, a look of relief on her face, "I didn't think you was faking that accent . . . but you never know."

Winking and glancing around the restaurant, Cassidy said, "You never really do . . . do you?"

FIFTEEN

I HAVE A DREAM
★ ★ ★

After three days on the beaches of Gulf Shores, Alabama, Cassidy headed north. He felt rested and refreshed by the sun and the cool waters of the Gulf. The war seemed to be gradually flaking off like dry skin after a sunburn, the memories now fading into an even deeper dimness. He felt himself rising out of the darkness.

Heading up Highway 31, he reached Montgomery at noon, stopping for lunch at a roadside cafe. Then, after a brief visit to the White House of the Confederacy, he continued north on 31 toward Birmingham. Driving into the city in the early afternoon, Cassidy felt a sense of unease, a kind of restlessness in the sultry and oppressive atmosphere. People bunched on street corners; others wore stoic masks behind their car windshields.

From his vantage point high atop Red Mountain, Vulcan, the largest cast-iron statue in the world, gazed down on Schloss Furnaces. Named after the god of fire and of metalworking in Roman mythology, the people of Birmingham thought it a fitting tribute to their iron and steel industry. Glancing at the distant statue, Cassidy suddenly felt a sense of foreboding, its glowering presence above the city calling to mind the title of a book he had seen recently, *The Fire Next Time*.

A restless night in a cheap motel, a big breakfast of smoked ham and eggs and buttered grits, and Cassidy found himself ready to see the town. He walked past the "Heaviest Corner on Earth," named after a group of skyscrapers built there shortly after the turn of the century, visited the old ironworks, then quickly lost interest in the history of Birmingham.

As he was returning to his car, Cassidy heard the sound of people shouting and a deep undertone of murmuring. A block away he found them marching along the street in the hot sunshine, their faces dark and glistening with sweat . . . and shining with hope. Martin Luther King led the group of men, women, and schoolchildren carrying signs proclaiming freedom and equal rights for all Americans.

Along the sidewalks, men and women wearing expressions of rage or outrage shouted insults, while others merely stared at the marchers, their expressions ranging from mild interest to tight-lipped disapproval. Policemen on foot and in patrol cars kept narrow-eyed watch on the procession.

Cassidy thought the whole thing was fascinating. As he watched from the sidewalk, a dark-skinned man with gray hair and an expression of pure joy walked past carrying a big brown Bible. He turned his smile on Cassidy.

Then the march ground to a halt, something up front out of sight delaying it. For no reason he could think of, Cassidy found himself stepping to the edge of the sidewalk next to the man with the dark suit and the bright smile.

"Y'all look like you're having a good time today," Cassidy said, surveying the crowd.

"Some of us is," the man said, glancing at the sidewalk lookers and the policemen, "and some of us ain't."

Cassidy stuck out his hand. "I'm Cassidy Temple."

"Pastor Buford Scott," he said, his teeth white in the dark face. "Mt. Zion Baptist Church."

Suddenly the sound of screaming and hoarse shouting rose from the front of the procession. As Cassidy watched, the people turned back against the line of march, fleeing something that pressed in on them. Men, women, and children gave way before the onslaught of uniformed men wearing helmets. Plastic face shields, glinting in the sunlight, hid their faces. In their black-gloved hands, they carried nightsticks and cattle prods.

"Looks like our fun's about over," Buford said, his voice freighted with resignation. He seemed unafraid, only weighed down by the years.

"I don't think y'all are doing anything so bad."

Buford turned his age-washed eyes on Cassidy. "I expect you don't. Only trouble is you ain't Bull Conner."

"Who's that?"

"Chief of Police here in Birmingham."

"Why do they call him 'Bull'?"

"You stick around here much longer, son," Buford said, glancing at the line of policemen advancing through the crowd, "you liable to find out." He turned toward the middle of the street. "Guess I'd better try to get some of these children out of the way 'fore they gets hurt."

Suddenly, a nightstick thudded across Buford's back, sending him to his knees. Cassidy leaped from the curb, reaching down to help him stand up. He felt something grip the back of his neck, pulling him upward. He whirled around, crouched in a defensive position. Instinctively, he considered the best way to disable the policeman facing him. Then he fought against the training that almost took over.

"Don't take on more than you can handle, sonny boy," the policeman growled. He had already summoned help with an unseen gesture.

"You be leavin' now, Mr. Temple," Buford groaned. "No sense in you gettin' in trouble over this."

As Cassidy turned again to help Buford up, he felt a sharp, thudding pain against the side of his head, then fell to his knees. Gloved hands wrestled his arms behind his back, cuffing his wrists together. In a daze, he felt himself dragged away.

His vision blurry, he saw Buford shoved along next to him, helpless in the hands of two burly policemen. Water splashing against his face sharpened his senses. In a haze of sunlight, he saw firemen turning high-pressure hoses on the crowd. Men in dark coveralls waded in, leading German shepherds on short leather leashes.

★ ★ ★

The common cell had been designed for twenty men. The day Cassidy was shoved into it along with Pastor Buford Scott, it held forty-two. A heavy metal table with built-in benches stood in the middle of the floor, its legs sunk into the bare concrete. Several benches extended from the block walls. The place smelled of unwashed bodies and fear. Shouts rang down the long halls. Off in the distance a radio not quite tuned to the station played "Blowin' in the Wind."

"Ain't you in a fine mess?" Buford sat on the floor next to Cassidy.

"I probably should have been in a place like this years ago." Gingerly rubbing the knot behind his right ear, Cassidy said, "My life was gettin' kinda dull anyway. This is just what I needed to spice it up a little."

Buford gazed around the crowded cell, then an infectious laugh rolled up out of his belly. Some of the other men laughed along with him even though they had no idea what it was all about. "My, my, my," Buford said, shaking his head.

"What's wrong?" Cassidy asked.

"The Good Lawd sho' got a sense of humor sticking you in here wid' de likes of us."

"You think God did this?"

Buford's eyes twinkled merrily. "Sho' I do. My Bible says that the steps of a righteous man are ordered by God. If you wudn't a righteous man, you sho' wouldn't a been out in dat street trying to help me."

Cassidy sensed that Buford was perfectly content sitting on a concrete floor in a smelly, crowded jail cell. He remembered that same quiet contentment in Caffey, even during those last hours just before going out on a mission into VC-occupied jungles. "Maybe I'm not as righteous as you think."

Buford's eyes searched Cassidy's. "You got a good heart, son. I can see that much."

"You think that's why they stuck me in this jail . . . because I've got a good heart?"

Buford smiled again. "You joking about it, but they's more truth to that than you think." He looked off into the distance. "You take ol' Paul. He was treated real good by the leaders of Israel long as he was giving Christians a hard time. But after Jesus changed his heart that day on the road to Damascus . . . and he started lovin' folks instead of hatin' 'em, look what happened to him then . . . he was beat, stoned, put in jail, shipwrecked, and snakebit."

"But he ran his race . . . and he finished his course," Cassidy added, surprised at his own words. Although he could not explain it, he felt a sudden lifting of the heaviness in his heart. The anger he had carried around for years, the heartache over Linda, the bitterness over his wounded eye; all the pain and the cares and the burdens seemed to be lifting, vanishing into the stale, sultry air of the Birmingham jail.

That's it! Cassidy thought with sudden realization as though a veil had been pulled aside. *God doesn't expect miracles from us. We don't have to be perfect to come to Jesus. He just wants us to come as we are . . . give Him our whole life . . . and He'll take care of everything else. And we don't have to see the heavens split open or hear choirs of angels singing to be saved. All we have to do is believe Jesus . . . and finish our race.*

"*That if thou shalt confess with thy mouth the Lord Jesus, and shalt believe in thine heart that God hath raised him from the dead, thou shalt be saved.*" The verse seemed to speak itself in Cassidy's mind. *All the years I've heard that, now I really know what it means. It's so simple!* When Cassidy came back from his own thoughts, he saw Buford gazing into his eyes.

"You already got Jesus in your heart, son," Buford said. "God just spoke to me about that. Now you need to tell somebody out loud."

Cassidy nodded his head.

"Will I do?" Buford grinned. "I ain't much," he glanced around the cell, "but then the pickin's is kinda slim right now."

"You'll do just fine."

Buford motioned with his hand and several of the men walked over and stood next to Cassidy.

Tears slipped down Cassidy's cheeks unnoticed. He became faintly aware of soothing warmth slowly building in his right eye. Kneeling on the concrete floor, he bowed his head, feeling callused, work-hardened hands placed on his shoulders as he began to pray, "Jesus . . ."

★ ★ ★

"You be sure and thank yo' daddy for what he done." Buford clasped Cassidy around the shoulders with his big hands. "If it wudn't for him, they might have locked me down *under* that jail like they did to po' ol' Paul over in Rome."

"You could have bonded out," Cassidy said, squinting into the late-afternoon sunlight. Standing in a park on top of Red Mountain, he gazed out over the city.

"Might not have been that easy." Buford shook his head. "I noticed the po-leese can slow things down a whole lot if they've got a mind to."

"Guess it didn't hurt to have a Louisiana state representative call the mayor's office."

Buford sat down on a concrete park bench in the shade of an elm. Pale gold sunlight slanted down through the leaves. "What you gonna do with yourself now?"

Cassidy sat down next to him. "What do you mean?"

"You startin' a whole new life now, son, a journey that started right down there in that jailhouse. You got a Bible?"

"At home."

Buford laughed, the sound of it rolling out of him like a river of joy. "Gonna be kinda hard to read it in Baton Rouge and you over here in Birmingham."

"I'll get another one tomorrow."

"Here, you can have this one," Buford offered, holding out his Bible, its brown leather cover worn thin.

"I can't take yours."

Buford looked genuinely hurt at Cassidy's refusal. "You ain't gonna let me be a blessing to my new brother in Christ?"

"It's just that . . ." Cassidy looked at the much used Bible. "It must mean a lot to you."

"It does." Buford's hand remained steady as he held the Bible toward Cassidy.

Looking for words that he couldn't seem to find, Cassidy simply took the Bible and held it, rubbing its smooth cover with the palm of his hand.

"You going back home now?"

Cassidy shook his head. "Not yet." He looked into Buford's thoughtful eyes. "I . . . I made a lot of mistakes, did a lot of things I shouldn't have . . . for a long time. There're a lot of people it's not going to be easy for me to face."

"Well, you'll get on back when the time is right. Paul went out in the desert by his self not long after he met Jesus on the road to Damascus. I expect he was gettin' things right in his head after Jesus did the work in his heart." Buford rubbed an abrasion on the back of his hand where it had scraped against the pavement during his arrest. "When I first got saved, I felt a lot like you do. Our pastor—what a great man of God he was—showed me some scripture from Isaiah. It's been a blessing to me all these years . . . and it might be to you, too."

Cassidy felt his mind turning from the things of the past as he listened to the words written seven centuries before the birth of Christ.

Buford closed his eyes and called back the scripture he had memorized as a young man. " 'Remember ye not the former things, neither consider the things of old. Behold, I will do a new thing; now it shall spring forth; shall ye not know it? I will even make a way in the wilderness, and rivers in the desert.' "

"What chapter is that in?"

Smiling, Buford opened his eyes and looked at Cassidy. "You'll find it . . . when you start searching the scriptures."

As Cassidy listened to the old preacher, the words seemed to reach down into his heart.

"Read your Bible every day," Buford began. "Pray as much as you can stand. Don't ever wait till you feel like it, cause the ol' devil will try to steal your friendship with Jesus if you do. A little 'Now I lay me down to sleep' prayer at night ain't gonna see you through the trials of this ol' world."

The light in Buford's eyes never failed, although the weariness of his body seeped into the sound of his voice. "Find yo'self a good Bible-believin' church." Then he grinned, his eyes crinkling at the corners. "Something else."

"What's that?"

"Love everybody. I know how silly that sounds to you now . . . did to me, too, at first."

"Sounds impossible."

"I know that, too," Buford said, and the peace deep inside his heart glowed in his face. "But the closer you get to Jesus, the easier it'll be."

Cassidy stared at the worn Bible clasped in his hands. "It seems so hard to do, Buford. I don't know if I can live a Christian life or not."

"You can't."

Cassidy turned a stunned expression on the old preacher. His mouth opened to ask, "Well, what's the use—"

"Nobody can. If we could have, Jesus wouldn't have had to come down here. But He did, and He done whipped that ol' devil at Calvary. The battle's already won. Not *you*, but '*Christ* in you, the hope of glory.'"

"It's kind of confusing."

"Don't try to understand everything with your head," Buford said, placing his hand on Cassidy's shoulder. "And whenever the ol' devil tries to put doubts in your head, you just remember that day in the Birmingham jail. Remember kneeling on that concrete floor; remember them ditchdiggers and concrete finishers laying their ol' rough hands on your shoulders; and remember how Jesus came into your heart that day."

Cassidy could almost feel the faith of Buford Scott flowing out of him like a river as he spoke.

Buford patted Cassidy's shoulder, then placed his arms on the bench and leaned back, staring at the pale blue sky slowly changing to lavender. "And when you get down or lonely or jes' get a dose of the blues, remember you got a friend who won't ever leave you or forsake you. His name is Jesus."

★ ★ ★

Cassidy left Birmingham that same night, traveling north through Chattanooga and on to Knoxville, where he got a job bagging groceries at an A&P, staying for a week in a boardinghouse. Then he was on the road again, his restless odyssey leading him further from the only life he had ever known. Every night alone in a rented room, he would open Buford's Bible and read. He came to regard it as a great treasure, its words burning in his heart one day, flowing through him like a quiet, peaceful river the next.

Each night and each morning Cassidy knelt beside his bed in prayer. At times he felt dry and empty and alone, but he held to these times of prayer. And when he thought the windows of heaven had been shut against him, still he kept praying. In those times he would often read in Psalms of the time when David had also felt deserted and cried out to God: "Hear my prayer, O Lord, and let my cry come unto thee. . . . For my days are consumed like smoke, and my bones are burned as an hearth. . . . My days are like a shadow that declineth; and I am withered like grass."

And always at an unexpected time, the river would come, refreshing him, filling him with strength and peace from its living waters.

★ ★ ★

Cassidy walked along the landscaped grounds near the main entrance of the Lincoln Memorial. Constructed of white Colorado marble and surrounded by a colonnade of thirty-six Greek Doric columns, one for each state at the time of Lincoln's death, it rose eighty feet against the blue summer sky. At the other end of the long reflecting pool toward the east stood the towering Washington Monument.

The crowd had been gathering all day in Potomac Park for the "March on Washington for Jobs and Freedom." Before the ceremony began, it would reach 250,000 people, spilling down the base of the Memorial composed of three immense marble platforms, out onto the wide terrace, along both sides of the reflecting pool, and into the trees that shaded the park grounds between the two great structures built in honor of America's first and sixteenth presidents.

Cassidy found a spot near the southwest corner of the pool. Sitting down on the ground, he leaned back against a tree trunk and opened his Bible. Soon he lost himself in its pages, the drone of the crowd all around him.

"You a preacher or something?"

Cassidy looked up at the young woman standing next to him. Her hair was a mass of tight black curls and her skin the color of café au lait. She wore a white cotton dress, gold-rimmed glasses, and an expression of bewilderment.

"Nope." Cassidy closed his Bible and stood up. "Why do you ask?"

"Well, you got that Bible for one thing, and you don't exactly blend in with the color scheme around here." She glanced about. "This crowd is heavy on the side of maids, busboys, and dishwashers. I don't figure you for any one of them."

Cassidy laughed, following her gaze. "I don't figure you for one, either."

Her dark liquid eyes flared with anger. "What do you know about me? You don't know nothin' about me or any of these people, white boy. I bet you ain't never worked a day in your pampered lily white life."

Cassidy found that he could still smile in spite of the venom being poured out on him from this total stranger. "Why are you so angry at me?"

The woman's face twisted with rage. "'Cause it's people like you who oppress the poor!"

"What do you know about me? You don't know nothin' about me." Cassidy did not endear himself to the woman by repeating her own words to her.

She stood there in front of him, hands clenched

into tight fists, speechless with anger.

"This man bothering you?" The voice sounding like a deep growl came from behind Cassidy. Its tall, dark-skinned owner wore a leather headband, tight black trousers, and open-toed sandals. Stepping defensively next to the girl, he asked her, "He trying to stir up trouble?"

"What else?"

The man glared at Cassidy's fatigue shirt with its twin chevrons on the sleeves. "You part of the military-industrial complex that's sucking the blood out of poor working people?"

Cassidy had seen one side of the civil rights movement in Birmingham in the person of Buford Scott. He was seeing a completely different side in Washington, D.C. "No."

The man grinned, but his eyes remained cold. "You been over in Vietnam killing women and babies?"

"No."

"You better just get on out of here. You ain't got no right to be with these people."

To his surprise, Cassidy felt no anger toward the man. He recalled times past when far less provocation than this would have turned loose the violence in him that had always seemed to lurk just below the surface. "I thought this whole movement was about equal rights for *everybody*." He glanced at the girl. "Maybe I was wrong."

The man stepped forward, towering over Cassidy, his fists clenched at his sides. "You better shut yo' mouth, cracker!" Then he looked into Cassidy's serene eyes and saw something that took the bluster out of him. There was absolutely no fear there, only a calmness and a confidence that shook him.

"Show him what we do with white trash that come up here making trouble," the girl urged her boyfriend.

The man seemed to know that this slim young man with the blue eyes and white hair would not be bluffed or bullied. Then he glanced at the corded muscles in Cassidy's tanned forearms and biceps, turned to the young woman, and said, "Ah, he ain't worth working up a sweat over."

As the couple walked away among the swelling crowd, Cassidy felt a sense of disappointment and disillusionment sweep over him. He had believed that the civil rights movement was necessary to end the injustice of bigotry and the persistent denial of basic rights to blacks. Now that he had seen the other side, he wondered if it would only evolve into a movement advocating the denial of these same rights to whites.

He hoped that the violence and hatred he had seen in the eyes of the young man and woman who had confronted him was the exception, and not the evidence of a dark and violent side to his nation's character, a spiritual viciousness that lay just beneath the glittering surface of material well-being.

Then, after a long list of speakers and singers and dignitaries had spent their allotted time before the microphone, Cassidy found some of his confidence in his nation's future returning as he listened to the words of the man everyone had come to hear.

"I have a dream that one day this nation will rise up and live out the true meaning of its creed . . . that all men are created equal. I have a dream. . . . So let freedom ring . . . And when this happens, when we let it ring, we will speed that day when all of God's children . . . will be able to join hands and sing in the words of the old Negro spiritual:

Free at last, free at last.

Thank God Almighty, we're free at last."

SIXTEEN

THE YEARS GONE BY

★ ★ ★

"May I help you find something?" The dapper young man peered at Cassidy over the top of his newspaper. His thin brown hair was as neat as the tightly knotted blue tie and laundered white shirt. "We don't get many customers in this early."

"I run almost every morning," Cassidy replied, glancing at the stacks and shelves and displays of books. "Thought I'd just browse around for a while."

Ignoring Cassidy's remarks, the man got up and ushered him over to a display. "Here's something that's been a hot seller. James Baldwin's *The Fire Next Time.*"

Cassidy remembered the title coming to mind back in Birmingham when he had seen the statue of Vulcan staring out over the city. "No thanks."

"The title comes from a great line. 'God gave Noah the rainbow sign, no more water, the fire next time.' "

"A little too apocalyptic for me," Cassidy said, starting to turn away.

"Perhaps you're right." The man pointed to another

display near the front entrance. "If you prefer fiction, I'm sure you'll enjoy *Close to the Heart*. It's by a new author." He motioned for Cassidy to follow him. "She's a marvelous writer!"

Cassidy stood before the display, staring open-mouthed at his sister's picture on the slick cardboard ad. With her shy smile, clear brown eyes, and the soft, shining sweep of her hair, she looked like a girl from one of the Clairol shampoo ads.

"Sharon Temple. Have you heard of her?"

"What . . . oh yes, yes I have." In the six months since she had first told him, Cassidy had almost forgotten when her novel was to be published. "I'll take one."

"Excellent choice." The man snatched a novel from the shelf and walked to the counter, where he rang up the sale and slid the book into a black-and-white bag.

After paying for his book, Cassidy walked to a corner of the store and took a seat in an upholstered chair in a little sitting area furnished with a coffee service. He poured a cup of coffee, added sugar, and settled back in the soft chair.

"My little sister's a celebrity," he said softly. Opening the book, he read the synopsis and Sharon's brief bio on the inside cover, turning past the title and copyright pages. Then he saw the dedication:

> To Cassidy, my brother:
> There's an empty place
> In my heart.
> Come home.

Staring at the words his sister had penned for him, Cassidy knew that his time in the desert was past. He whispered, "I'm on my way, Sharon."

★ ★ ★

Caffey sat down heavily and stretched his legs out on the grass of the infield as he watched Cassidy finish a final wind sprint, his spikes flicking up gray dust clouds on the cinder track. Gazing beyond the bleachers toward the two-story building, Caffey remembered his friend slugging it out in the "Bull Pen" one cold February day with a twenty-year-old from New Orleans who had made the trip up to test his reputation.

Then he looked at Cassidy heading toward him. Since his return, Caffey had never seen him lose his temper, never seen the icy light in his blue eyes that had always presaged fury and mayhem. *You've really changed, Cass*, he thought, then said, "God ol' Istrouma."

Breathing heavily, Cassidy sprawled next to his friend. "You really miss this place, don't you?"

"Yep," Caffey admitted. "We had some good times here." He turned his gaze toward the past. "I miss the pep rallies before the football games and the first cold weather when we could wear our letter jackets . . . and all the pretty girls laughing and talking a mile a minute." Clearing his throat, he continued. "But I don't think about it as much as I used to since I stared working out at LSU. I really like my job."

"Why are you goin' back to school then?" Cassidy's face glistened with sweat. He wiped it with a white towel, then rubbed his damp hair.

"We've done everything else together all these years, so we might as well finish track together. I'm not sweatin' out here in this August sunshine 'cause I like it, that's for sure." Caffey blinked in the slanting light. "Think we can still cut it on the team?"

Cassidy shrugged. "The army kept us in pretty good shape, but it's still gonna take a lot of work. After all, we're gettin' to be old men now."

"Twenty-one ain't old," Caffey said with a grin, then

he lay on is back, staring up at the pale sky of late summer. "My boss told me if I'd major in agriculture he'd let me supervise the dairy program after I graduate. You know, all the silos and barns and milking sheds . . . the whole works."

"Sounds good. You like animals."

"Yeah, I really do. I'd get to work the rodeos and the livestock shows, too."

Cassidy pulled the towel around his neck, gripping the ends with both hands. "I heard there was a little brown-eyed girl working at the campus ice cream store who had something to do with you going back to school."

"Who told you that?" Caffey sat up quickly, color rising in his thick neck.

"Sharon mentioned it."

"Shoot!" Caffey shook his head slowly. "Can't tell a woman nothing without the whole town knowing it."

"Just me, Caffey. She didn't tell anybody else," Cassidy said. "I'm your best friend. Guess she figured it was all right."

"Yeah, well . . . I guess it is," he admitted reluctantly. A smile crept slowly across this broad, honest face. "She's real nice, Cass. Her name's Alice, and she makes me feel . . . *good* just walking along next to me. I think you'd really like her."

"Well . . ."

Caffey came out of his mild trance. "Well, what?"

"When can I meet her?"

Cassidy's smile widened another half-inch. "She's coming to church with me Sunday."

"Good. I'll have to give my approval before this romance goes any further."

"You'll approve." Caffey gave Cassidy a reflective glance, then began plucking blades of grass from the ground between his legs. "Guess who came by to see me this morning?"

"Beats me."

"Warren Barbay."

"No kiddin'?" Cassidy leaned forward, elbows resting on his knees.

Caffey chewed on a blade of grass as he spoke. "He told me a strange story."

Cassidy stared past the bleachers at the baseball diamond. Several grade-school boys wearing jeans and T-shirts chose up sides and started a noisy game.

"Barbay said you went to his house last week . . . asked him to forgive you for what you did to him."

Nodding, Cassidy kept his eyes on the game.

"He's kinda worried that you're up to something."

Cassidy turned toward Caffey. "Why?"

Grinning, Caffey spit out the grass and said, "He told me he thinks you've gone crazy."

"I guess he would at that," Cassidy laughed. He stood up, offered Caffey his hand, and pulled him to his feet. "Let's go to the house and get two big glasses of Mama's iced tea."

"Sounds good to me." Caffey placed his big paw on Cassidy's shoulder as they walked toward the parking lot. "You know what, ol' buddy?"

"What's that?"

"I'm sure glad we had that fight in the fifth grade."

★ ★ ★

Catherine heard the sound of the kitchen door opening. "I'm in the living room, Cass."

Cassidy dumped his stack of books on the table and walked down the hall to join her.

Looking away from the black-and-white images on the television screen, she saw the sorrow etched on her son's face. "You've heard. . . ."

Nodding, Cassidy sat on the couch next to his mother. "I was walking across the quadrangle to my one o'clock class when somebody told me."

"Such a terrible tragedy! Jacqueline and those two precious children." Catherine realized that she spoke as though she actually knew the family.

Cassidy stared blankly at the television screen. "Everybody was gathering in front of the library after they heard the news." He shook his head sadly. "Some were crying; some looked like they were almost in shock. I guess most of us were just stunned; it hadn't really registered yet. And one or two said they were glad he was dead." Looking at Catherine, he continued. "And they meant it, too. . . . I could see it in their faces."

"It's awful, Cass, but the country will survive it." Catherine's words sounded to her as though they were coming from somewhere far away as she spoke them. "We survived the Civil War and Lincoln's assassination . . . and all these other wars. We'll make it through this, too."

They sat together in the quiet November afternoon while the drama in Dallas played out before them on the television screen. Outside the window in the wind, autumn-dry leaves scraped along the sidewalk.

"You look tired," Catherine said finally.

"I'm okay."

"I'm glad to see you spending so much time helping out with the youth group at church, but you're carrying a full schedule in school and working out with the track team. I don't think you're getting enough rest."

"I've wasted too many years already, Mama. Gotta make up for lost time."

Catherine blew a wisp of pale hair back from her face. "You know what the pastor told me?"

Clasping his hands behind his head, Cassidy leaned

against the back of the couch. "That I'm a prince of a fellow and an all-around good guy?"

"Better than that."

Cassidy tried to feign disinterest, then turned his head toward his mother. After a few more seconds of silence, he sat up. "Well, what did he say?"

"Hmm . . ." Catherine rubbed her temple with her fingertips. "Why, I believe I've forgotten."

"Ah, c'mon, Mama."

"Well, let me see now." She gazed at Cassidy's eager expression, a silent prayer of thanksgiving rising in her spirit that his right eye was now as clear and normal as the left. "First of all, he was sincerely impressed by your talk to the youth last Wednesday night."

Cassidy nodded. "I didn't even know what I was going to say when I got up there. He just asked me at the last minute."

"I think he planned it that way, Cass." As Catherine gazed at her son, she silently thanked God for the miraculous change in his life. "And he told me he thinks God has called you to preach."

"He did?"

"He surely did."

"You know something, Mama?" Cassidy leaned back again, gazing off into the distance. "All I did was tell them about what Jesus has done in my life . . . and two girls and a boy came down to the altar afterwards. Gave their hearts to Jesus right there. I was more surprised than anybody in the whole place."

"Maybe it's because they've seen the change in your life." A faint smile gathered at the corners of Catherine's mouth. "I expect most of them have heard the stories about you, Cass . . . your youthful indiscretions."

Cassidy slipped his brown loafers off and stretched out on the long couch. "That's an understatement. I've finally realized that the good Lord was looking out for me all those years . . . and I wasn't even thinking about Him."

Catherine got up and turned the television off. Returning to her place on the couch, she watched Cassidy, his eyes closed, his breathing becoming slow and regular as he quickly dropped off to sleep. She called back the day eighteen years before when she had gotten the news that the war was over and Lane would be coming home to her. She saw Cass again as a three-year-old, asleep on the sofa in a golden swatch of sunlight, the long white curtains blowing into the room. Outside the window, the wind stirred the pale, graceful sweep of the weeping willow boughs. The leaves shimmered and swayed and brushed softly against the screen as though sighing an arboreal lullaby to the sleeping child inside. And she could almost hear again the bittersweet lyrics of "I'll Be Seeing You" playing on the radio:

I'll find you in the morning sun and when the night is new. . . .

Catherine came slowly back to the present. She gazed at Cassidy, her prodigal son at last come home . . . and she believed that God was going to do great things in his life. Bowing her head, she gave thanks to her Father for His blessings and His faithfulness, for her family, for seeing them through all the dark times.

★ ★ ★

In a hospital emergency room in Dallas, a grim-faced man in a rumpled suit gathered his fallen President's clothes together for safeguarding. As he picked up the jacket, a folded sheet of paper fell out. Picking it up he saw that it contained notes for the speech the President was to give that day. Silently, he read a portion of the speech.

We are in this country . . . watchmen on the walls of freedom. . . . We ask, therefore, that we . . . may achieve the ancient vision of peace on earth, goodwill toward men.